Kathleen's Unforgettable Winter

BOOK TWO
of the
A Life of Faith: Kathleen McKenzie
Series

TRACY LEININGER CRAVEN

MCP
Mission City Press
Franklin, Tennessee

Book Two of the *A Life of Faith: Kathleen McKenzie* Series

Kathleen's Unforgettable Winter
Copyright © 2006, Tracy Leininger Craven. All Rights Reserved.

Published by Mission City Press, Inc.

Cover & Interior Design: Richmond & Williams
Typesetting: BookSetters

Unless otherwise indicated, all Scripture references are from the Holy Bible, New International Version (NIV). Copyright © 1973, 1978, 1984 by International Bible Society. Used by permission of Zondervan Publishing House, Grand Rapids, MI. All rights reserved.

Kathleen McKenzie and *A Life of Faith* are trademarks of Mission City Press, Inc. For more information, write to Mission City Press at 202 Second Avenue South, Franklin, Tennessee 37064, or visit our Web Site at: **www.alifeoffaith.com.**

For a FREE catalog call 1-800-840-2641.

Library of Congress Catalog Card Number: 2006930437
Craven, Tracy Leininger
        Kathleen's UnforgettableWinter
        Book Two of the *A Life of Faith: Kathleen McKenzie* Series
        ISBN-13: 978-1-928749-26-4
        ISBN-10: 1-928749-26-7

Printed in the United States of America
3 4 5 6 7 8 — 11 10 09 08

DEDICATION

To my husband, David, for his unfailing love and support and to our precious daughter Elaina Hope.

AMERICAN FARM LIFE IN THE 1930s

*F*arm life in rural America in the 1930s was still quite primitive for most farmers. The majority of homes did not have running water or electricity, which meant life without telephones, radios, air-conditioning, and refrigerators. If you lived on a farm you most likely bathed in a tin tub with water heated on the wood-burning stove. On a cold winter day, when you used the bathroom, you ran outside to the outhouse. At night, instead of flipping a light switch to illuminate the room, you used a candle or lantern to see.

Housework took much longer without washing machines, vacuum cleaners, and electric stoves. Farming wasn't as efficient. Cows had to be milked by hand, and even though tractors and other large farming equipment had been invented, most farmers didn't have the money to buy such fancy machinery. The "horse power" they plowed their fields with was from their faithful four-hoofed steeds or oxen.

Many folks still used a horse and wagon to travel to town instead of investing in a car and buying gasoline. In many ways, life for the McKenzie family at Stonehaven Farm echoed the lifestyle of the pioneers who lived off the land.

1930 AMERICAN ECONOMY OVERVIEW: THE YEAR AFTER THE STOCK MARKET CRASH

Though the stock market crash of October, 1929 didn't affect everyone immediately, especially those living on farms, there was definitely a trickle-down effect that began to touch more and more lives over the next year. In 1930, 1,352 banks failed, losing over $853 million. This meant that honest working men who had their life savings in accounts at one of those banks lost everything. In the same year, 26,355 businesses closed, and the value of all farm property and crop prices declined considerably.[1] Millions lost their jobs, and though President Hoover claimed that "no one is going hungry," thousands of homeless were beginning to live in communities of shacks they built out of scrap wood, cardboard, and whatever else they could find to shelter themselves. People called these communities "Hoovervilles."

[1] *The Great Depression, America in the 1930s* by T. H. Watkins, Back Bay Books, page 55.

McKenzie Family Tree

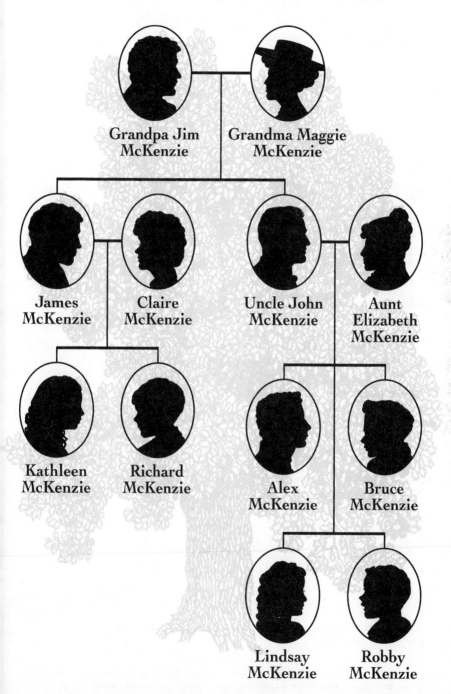

SETTING

The story begins New Year's Day, 1930. Kathleen and her family are traveling to Archbold, Ohio, to live with their relatives at Stonehaven, the McKenzie family farm, until Kathleen's father, James McKenzie, is able to find a steady job.

CHARACTERS

∞ THE McKENZIE HOUSEHOLD ∞

James McKenzie — Age 35, Kathleen's father
Claire McKenzie — Age 32, Kathleen's mother.
Their children:
> **Kathleen McKenzie** — Age 12
> **Richard McKenzie** — Age 9

Grandma Maggie and Grandpa Jim McKenzie — Kathleen's grandparents
Aunt Elizabeth and Uncle John McKenzie — Kathleen's aunt and uncle, and their children:
> **Alex** — Age 18, Kathleen's cousin
> **Bruce** — Age 15, Kathleen's cousin
> **Lindsay** — Age 14, Kathleen's cousin
> **Robby** — Age 8, Kathleen's cousin

∞ OTHERS ∞

Lucy Meier — Age 12, Kathleen's best friend in Fort Wayne, Indiana
Peter Meier — Age 14, Lucy's brother

Dr. and Mrs. Schmitt — Family doctor and his wife, friends of the McKenzies and parents of:

> **Freddie Schmitt** — Schoolmate and friend of Kathleen

Mr. and Mrs. Johnston — Neighbors and owner of the dog Old Bruiser

The Williams family — New family to the community that just moved to Ohio from the South

Stonehaven

*Therefore, if anyone is in Christ, he is a new creation;
the old has gone, the new has come!*
2 CORINTHIANS 5:17

Snow crunched underneath Kathleen McKenzie's boots as she walked to the back of the car and placed a basket of food in the trunk of the white Chevy sedan. She shivered in the frosty morning air and wrapped her wool coat tighter around her. The sun was not due to rise for at least an hour as she and her family packed the last of their belongings for their move to her grandparents' farm in Ohio. She climbed in the backseat next to her brother, Richard. It was warmer inside the car. She was grateful that their new car had a heater.

Papa backed out of the driveway and the car headlights shone on their home. Kathleen took one last look before it disappeared from sight. A sad, empty feeling swept over her.

"Good-bye, house," said Richard, waving his mittened hand. "Good-bye, Fort Wayne, Indiana." He flopped back in his seat, his frown reflecting how Kathleen felt.

Kathleen tucked the strand of red hair that was always falling into her eyes back under her wool hat. She had lived in the same house her whole life. It was not just their home that Kathleen would miss, but their church, her school, and her friends—especially Lucy, her best friend in the whole world. They'd had so much fun the past several months, playing and sharing secrets in Kathleen's tree house in Kirk's Woods. She'd never forget their last conversation. It had been just a week ago, after Papa had told her they were moving to his family's farm until he could find a steady job. Papa's boss had to close his construction business after he lost all his money when the stock market crashed several months before. This left Papa and all the other employees out of work. Papa had looked hard for work, but jobs were scarce.

It all seemed so dreadful, and she'd raced off to her favorite place to be by herself. Lucy had found her there, and in her kind, gentle way gave Kathleen a fresh perspective.

"I'm sure that there will be plenty of exciting experiences ahead that you can't even imagine," Lucy had said. "Living on a farm without electricity and plumbing is quite unique . . . and soon, you will be back home in Fort Wayne, and you can tell me all about the exciting times you had."

Kathleen smiled as she remembered. Lucy always chose to look on the bright side of life instead of dwelling on the negative. Hard as it was in this situation, Kathleen determined to do the same thing. Besides, maybe Lucy was right. Papa might find a job soon and then they could move back home—maybe in a month or less.

They drove past a sign that read, "Leaving Fort Wayne."

Dear God, please help me to trust that this will all turn out well and that Papa will find a job so we can come back home quickly.

"Mama, how far is it to Ohio?" asked Richard, leaning over the front seat.

"We should be there before lunchtime," said Mama, turning to look at them. By now the car was warm, and she took off her hat and gloves and coat and had Richard and Kathleen do the same.

"You children relax," said Papa, "maybe get some sleep. It'll make the trip go faster."

Kathleen couldn't imagine sleeping. She was determined to stay awake the entire drive. But before long the battle between the warm car, the soft leather seats, and the constant lull of the engine overpowered her resolve, and Kathleen nodded off to sleep.

She awoke to the sun shining brightly on her face. Kathleen sat up and looked out the window. As far as she could see, fields, lightly covered in a thin blanket of glinting snow, stretched in all directions.

Kathleen's Unforgettable Winter

Kathleen wondered if anyone lived in this new world they were traveling through. Then she spotted a red barn with a tall red-and-silver silo standing out like a beacon on the horizon.

"There! Off in the distance! Is that Stonehaven, Grandpa McKenzie's farm?" Kathleen was so excited to see signs of life that her voice was a bit louder than she expected.

Richard, who had been curled up asleep, bolted upright. "What did you say? Are we at the farm?" His voice sounded sleepy and he rubbed his eyes.

"Well, for gracious sakes, I thought my children would never wake up." Mama turned around to look at them from the front seat. "Your papa and I had almost given up hope."

"I don't want to disappoint the two of you," Papa said, never taking his gaze from the road, "but I'm afraid with the roads as icy as they have been this morning it will take us at least two more hours to get to the farm."

"The good thing about the long drive is it will give us plenty of time to be together with just our family," Mama said. "As you know, Grandpa and Grandma's house is quite small, and I am afraid we will not all fit into their one guest room."

What was Mama saying? Why hadn't Kathleen been told this before? "Where will we live then?" Kathleen asked. She remembered a few things about the old farmhouse, like the bright pink quilt with daisies

on the guest room bed. But most of the memories of Stonehaven had faded long ago.

"Well, I'm not totally sure," said Papa, "but my guess would be that your mama, Richard, and I will be staying at Grandma and Grandpa's, and you will probably end up living at Uncle John's with your cousin Lindsay. That's the house I grew up in. Grandpa didn't build the house they live in now until after Uncle John married, moved into the original homestead, and raised his family there." Papa looked at Kathleen through the rear-view mirror and smiled. "You never know, you may even get to sleep in the same room that I did when I was a lad."

"You mean we won't even be living in the same house!" Kathleen sat up straight and grabbed the seat in front of her. This was terrible news. Not be with her family?

"I know, honey," said Mama, patting her hand. "I would prefer we were all together too. Over the next few months, we will have to be flexible."

"Mama, I don't want to be away from you and Papa." Kathleen could hear the despair in her own voice.

"Now, Kathleen, it's not all that bad. Your uncle's house is just a stone's throw from Grandma and Grandpa's, and all the meals are cooked and served at Uncle John's, so we will be together — most of the day."

Most of the day? What did that mean? Kathleen had visions of being sent to live with another family and hardly ever seeing her papa and mama or Richard. This wasn't what she had pictured when she'd signed up for this adventure.

Kathleen's Unforgettable Winter

"You'll probably sleep with Lindsay, and I'm sure you both will get along marvelously."

She couldn't even remember Lindsay, and she was two years older than Kathleen. What would they have in common?

Mama must've seen the concern on her face. "If not, you're more than welcome to sleep on the floor with Richard in our room."

That didn't sound very inviting either. Kathleen sat back in her seat. Sleeping with someone she didn't know or sleeping on the floor? Which was worse?

"I'm sure I'll be fine sleeping at Uncle John's." Kathleen tried to sound cheerful, but life was changing too fast. She'd never had to share a room with anyone before. And the only older girls her cousin's age that she'd ever spent time with had not been very kind at all.

Kathleen had been five the last time she visited Uncle John and Aunt Elizabeth. Lindsay had hardly spoken a word to her. As hard as she tried, she could not remember what her cousin even looked like. Would they like each other? Would Lindsay mind sharing a room with her? Would they become close friends?

Her other cousins, Alex and Bruce, were even older than Lindsay. Alex would be eighteen now and full grown and Bruce nearly so. When she'd last seen Bruce he'd played a mean trick on her. Would he do something like that again?

16

Robby, her youngest cousin, was just a baby. She was going to live in a house of strangers. Would they accept a girl from the city?

Dear God, please help me fit in. I want them to like me, and I want to like them.

Kathleen tried to keep her mind off her worries by watching out the window, but all she saw were fields of snow and an occasional farm. Everyone was quiet for some time.

Richard broke the silence, "Papa, please tell us some stories of life on the farm when you were my age."

Kathleen leaned forward, eager to hear Papa's stories of growing up on the family farm with his three brothers—Uncle John, Uncle Joe, and Uncle William. Most of them made Kathleen laugh; she enjoyed hearing about how they rode the calves and got bucked off, ate green apples until they were sick to their stomachs, and put the teacher's bathtub on the roof of the schoolhouse as a prank.

"Did I ever tell you about the wolves?" he asked.

"No, Papa," said Richard, his eyes wide with excitement.

"James, don't scare the children." Mama shook her head.

"Tell me, tell me," said Richard, bouncing on the seat.

Mama gave Papa a withering look, but he continued, "When I was a boy, the wolves used to stalk along the wooded riverbanks . . ."

17

Kathleen's Unforgettable Winter

A chill ran down Kathleen's arms.

"Are there still wolves in Ohio, Papa?" Richard asked. Kathleen sensed that he was as frightened as she was by the idea of a wild animal sneaking up and attacking her when she least expected it.

"James, look, you've frightened Richard," Mama whispered as she gently nudged Papa's arm. "You'll give him nightmares."

"Oh, he knows I'm just kidding." Papa laughed. "Son, that was a long time ago. When I was a boy, wolves were as scarce as hens' teeth." He winked. "But when your Grandpa McKenzie came over from Scotland to settle this land, it was still wild and fierce. The wolves were such a threat that it was not safe for children to walk after dark to the barn or even to the outhouse. Mostly, the wolves just devoured the live-stock. But when the winter months grew long and cold, they were a threat to humans too. It didn't take long until the settlers in the area knew they must put a stop to it. Your grandpa was one of the brave men that went out and hunted them. When the last wolf was finally shot, the whole county held a huge celebration. A few people have claimed sighting a wolf since then, but no one has been able to produce any proof."

"I want to see a wolf!" Richard pretended to aim down his hand as if it were a revolver. "I'd shoot it dead before it even smelled me."

Kathleen shivered. "I don't want to see a wolf—ever! Are you sure they are all gone?" Kathleen had read

accounts of wolf encounters with early American mountain men and settlers. Those stories made the large animals sound extremely ferocious, just as Papa had said.

"I'm with you, Kathleen," said Mama. "I'd rather not see a wolf—or even hear one for that matter."

Nearly an hour past noon, they reached the top of a small hill, giving them a view of the flat, snow-covered, rolling farmland for miles around.

They had driven for a long time and had seen few buildings. Kathleen felt like they were out in the middle of nowhere. She hadn't seen any stores, banks, churches, or schools for miles. Where would she and Richard go to school? How would she mail a letter to Lucy like she'd promised?

"There's Stonehaven, the old homestead!" Papa said excitedly, pointing at a large green barn with white trim. Next to the barn rose a tall green silo. Not far from it stood a nice-sized, white two-story farmhouse with a porch that wrapped around the front and side.

Kathleen saw that there was a smaller white house nestled behind the bigger one. As they drove closer, she recognized many of the smaller buildings that dotted the farmyard and remembered the welcoming smell of the smokehouse, her fear of the large rooster that strutted around like he ruled the barnyard, and the unwelcome

memory of Bruce locking her in the frozen outhouse during the thick of winter.

Between the two houses towered a maple tree. Its bare branches stretched out almost as far as it was tall. A rope swing hung from one of its larger limbs. At first, Kathleen thought the tree looked stark and menacing against the backdrop of the white world that surrounded it; but then she thought how lovely its shade would be in the hot summer sun and decided it did not look so grim after all.

In the front yard of the larger farmhouse grew two smaller trees that looked quite dead. She was glad the house had cheerful green trim around the windows, or else every sign of life and color would have been buried three feet deep beneath the snow until spring.

Of course, they would not be here long enough to see it. Surely they would be safely back in Fort Wayne by then.

Papa drove up the icy driveway. The sound of the car engine must have alerted the family that they had arrived, because all of a sudden the entire homestead came to life.

The outhouse door flew open and a little boy burst out, tightening his belt as he ran. He looked to be about seven, with red curls and a face full of freckles. It had to be Robby. He did not seem to be in the least bit shy. He jumped up and down and waved, overjoyed to see them. At first Kathleen thought that he must have just been in a tussle with the dog or something else because his hair was shooting straight up in the front. But as he

20

came closer, she realized that Robby had a stubborn cowlick on his forehead—just like hers.

"Look at that cowlick—it's in the same place as mine," exclaimed Kathleen. "I'm sure glad that my hair is long, or it would probably stick up just like his." Kathleen pointed toward Robby. "And that red hair? He's definitely a McKenzie."

"There's my bonnie mither!" Papa said, putting on his thick Scottish accent.

On the front porch of the larger house, Grandma Maggie stood, waving eagerly with a dish towel. Her sweet round face was framed with lightly curled wisps of silvery white hair that had escaped from her loosely tied bun.

A woman who looked a lot like Mama stood next to her; it had to be Aunt Elizabeth. She had her arm wrapped around Grandma's waist. Her smile was warm and welcoming.

Two strong, broad-shouldered young men with pitchforks in hand appeared at the barn loft window. Bruce and Alex. They tossed the pitchforks aside and jumped out the second-floor window, disappearing for a second in the lush pile of hay they had been tossing down to the cows below.

"Did you see that?" said Richard, tugging on Kathleen's sleeve. "Boy, oh boy, does that look fun! I can't wait to help with the barn chores."

Grandpa, axe in hand, strode from around the house where the woodpile was. His face was weathered and

tanned from years of working in the sun, and his hands were strong and scarred, but his smile was kind and caring and his eyes were gentle. Uncle John, who looked a little like Papa, emerged out of the barn with a grin that looked broader than his shoulders—which were quite broad from years of hard farm labor.

Finally, Kathleen spotted a girl with waist-length blonde braids coming out of the barn. It had to be Lindsay. But what was she wearing? A pair of patched men's overalls! Kathleen had never in her life seen a girl in overalls. In fact, the only time she had ever seen a girl in anything but a dress was during PE at school or some other athletic event, but never in normal everyday life. However funny Lindsay was dressed, Kathleen hoped they would become good friends; after all, they were going to share the same bed.

Papa stopped the car. Kathleen's heart beat quickly as she opened the door. She was anxious to reacquaint herself with her cousins. She wondered if they would be happy to have her living under the same roof.

Dear God, please take away any fear I have of meeting my cousins. Help us to be friends.

2

A Surprise at the Farm

The boundary lines have fallen for me in pleasant places;
surely I have a delightful inheritance.

PSALM 16:6

Later that evening after supper, Lindsay led Kathleen upstairs to her bedroom so she could unpack her things. Lindsay lit a candle and its light flickered and danced on the wall, casting shadows about the room. The dim lighting created a cozy feeling, but Kathleen couldn't help but think how different it was from her room in Fort Wayne, where she just turned on a light switch. Kathleen wondered how she would ever be able to read or study her homework in the dusky candlelight.

"Are all your dresses this fancy?" Lindsay held up a lavender silk dress. She softly fingered the delicate lace collar.

23

"Goodness no! That's my Sunday best." Kathleen pointed to a pile of school dresses she had just placed on Lindsay's bed. "These are my everyday clothes."

"Those are your everyday clothes? What do you wear to work in?" Lindsay's face showed surprise.

"Is—is there something wrong with them?" Kathleen felt her cheeks growing warm. Her clothes were what everyone wore in Fort Wayne. She never thought anything about them before. What was Lindsay talking about? She placed her harmonica and Marguerite, the doll that she had received for her last birthday, on her cousin's nightstand.

"There's nothing wrong except they'll get awfully dirty working here on the farm." Lindsay shook her head as she opened her armoire. "You're welcome to store them here in my dresser."

Kathleen's cheeks began to burn as she hung her dresses in Lindsay's almost empty armoire. Her cousin only had two dresses hanging inside—one very plain, worn-out orange-and-red-checked dress and one nicer dress with pink and yellow flowers. No wonder Lindsay wore overalls all day and only changed into a dress for dinner. Was that why she was saying those things about her dresses? Did Lindsay think she was a spoiled city girl?

Kathleen suddenly realized how blessed she was to own so many clothes. She felt ashamed that she had always taken it for granted and never thought to thank God for things in her life like clothes and shoes.

Kathleen wished she could share with Lindsay, but her cousin looked to be at least two sizes bigger.

"Seems a waste to have so many dresses, if you ask me," said Lindsay, who was now looking at Marguerite as if she'd never seen anything like her before either. "Do you play with this doll or is she just a decoration?" she asked.

Was there a hint of mockery in her voice? "Ah, well," Kathleen suddenly felt younger than her older cousin. "She's special. I got her for my birthday."

"She sure is pretty." Lindsay stroked her silky hair. "I don't have much time for play. I'm too busy with my chores."

Kathleen looked around the bare room and realized that there were precious few things for girls to play with and no books. She wondered where Lindsay kept all her reading material.

"So what sort of work is there to do on the farm?" Kathleen asked, trying to divert Lindsay's attention from her things.

"You'll see in the morning." Lindsay yawned and began to undo her long braids. The candlelight flickering around the room made her hair shine like gold.

Kathleen finished unpacking and changed into her nightgown. She pondered all Lindsay had said as she brushed a strand of her light red hair until it was smooth and shiny, wrapped the ends around a thin, long piece of cloth, rolled it under until it was snug against her head, and then tied the ends of the rag to keep it in

25

place. What would the upcoming days be like here on the farm?

"Do all the girls in the big city wear their hair shoulder-length with curls like yours?" Lindsay asked from the bed where she was already buried under a mound of quilts.

"Not everyone. Lots of girls do, but some cut their hair much shorter and wear it straight or slightly curled at the end. They call it a 'bob'."

"Seems like a lot of work to me."

Kathleen heard her words, but she caught a hint of envy too. She wondered if Lindsay would like to curl her hair like this sometime. Maybe when they knew each other better, she could wrap her hair for her. It might look nice all curled up. Somehow, she didn't think tonight was a good time to bring up the subject.

Her first night with Lindsay felt very much like they were reading out of two different books. She wondered if they'd ever get on the same page and become friends like Lucy and she.

Uncle John came up the stairs and told them they had better get some sleep. "Morning will be here before you know it, and talking all night won't help a bit when it comes time to do all your chores bright and early."

Kathleen blew out the candle and snuggled deeply beneath the warmth of the quilts. She put her feet on the warm stone at the end of the bed, something she'd never done before and thought was rather odd at first,

but now was glad of its warmth. Lindsay lay beside her, her breathing steady. Was she already asleep?

Kathleen felt like she had gotten to know her a little bit from their conversations. She had discovered that her cousin preferred barn chores and riding her horse over dressing up for church socials. She was the opposite of Lucy, who liked tea parties, sewing, and playing with dolls. Lindsay also seemed not to care that there was a whole world outside of the boundary of their farm. Whenever Kathleen had brought up Fort Wayne, Lindsay had quickly changed the subject. Kathleen closed her eyes.

Dear God, I miss my friends; I miss my home. Please take the lonely feeling out of my heart. Help me to be strong and to look at my time here at Stonehaven as an adventure.

The next morning when Kathleen awoke, it was still pitch black outside. She wrapped the blankets tightly about her, but it was too cold to get back to sleep. She heard someone stirring downstairs in the kitchen. Kathleen shivered as she felt around in the dark for a match to light the candle. Once it was lit, she quickly dressed in her warmest wool dress, then grabbed her Bible and the candlestick off the nightstand. She glanced at Lindsay, who still slept peacefully, and briskly walked downstairs.

Aunt Elizabeth was stoking the wood-burning stove that had been in the family since Kathleen's Papa was a boy. Grandma Maggie affectionately referred to it as her

"old Mary Washington." Aunt Elizabeth looked up when Kathleen walked in. "You're up early!"

Kathleen eyed the bright red coals in the bottom of the stove and moved a little closer. "The upstairs bedroom was too cold for me to sleep, so as soon as I heard you moving around in the kitchen, I decided I'd come join you." Kathleen shivered. She placed her Bible on the kitchen table and held her hands out toward the warm stove. The warmth felt good.

"I'm so sorry, dear. Tonight I'll make sure that Lindsay gets another quilt out of the cedar chest. If you are still cold tomorrow morning, I'll have Bruce or Alex wake up in the middle of the night and warm up a stone to put at your feet."

Kathleen smiled. Last night was the first time she had ever slept with an oven-warmed stone at her feet. She had read in her history books about American settlers using stones in their beds to keep them warm, but Kathleen never imagined that people still used that ancient method for warmth. It worked wonderfully though, and Kathleen slept marvelously—that is, until she woke early that morning with a cold stone at her feet and the worst case of shivers she had ever experienced.

"Thank you, Aunt Elizabeth. I'm sure I'll be fine with the extra quilt." She didn't want to make Alex or Bruce get up in the middle of the night. She didn't imagine that would make them too happy with her. "I'm afraid I'm not much of a farm girl. I've never lived without a furnace heating the house. Papa says I'll soon

28

adjust. I'm sure I will. I just know that I will love it here—but I do think some things will be rather awkward for me at first." Kathleen surprised herself at how easily she fell into conversation with her aunt. Was it because of her kindhearted personality or because she looked so much like her mama?

Last night at supper Grandpa McKenzie had teased that all his boys thought their own mama was so beautiful that they had married women who looked just like her—with blue eyes and blonde hair. Of course, Grandma McKenzie's hair was now as white as snow, but Grandpa said when she was a bonnie young bride, she looked just like her daughters-in-law. And then Grandpa added, with a wink at Grandma, that his sons had taste almost as good as his.

Kathleen watched curiously as Aunt Elizabeth put a pail of ice on the stove. "Why is the water frozen?"

Aunt Elizabeth laughed. "That, my dear, is the reason why you couldn't sleep! It is so cold that the pail of water Alex fetched last night from the pump has frozen."

"You mean that pail of water froze while it was inside?" Kathleen had never heard of such a thing. That meant it must have gotten below freezing *inside* the house. She inched closer to the stove, welcoming its heat.

"Yes, I'm afraid we have some frigid days ahead of us."

Did that mean it was going to get colder? Kathleen could hardy imagine. She turned around to let her back warm. She promised herself never to take the furnace back home in Indiana for granted ever again.

Footsteps resounded down the stairs. She expected little Robby to come through the doorway, but it was Lindsay. "Good morning," she called sleepily. She wore a red plaid shirt under a pair of overalls, and her hair was already done up in braids.

"Looks like your cousin is the early bird," Aunt Elizabeth said as she looked from Lindsay to Kathleen. "Hopefully, you will rub off on Lindsay before school starts next week. She loves to sleep in — especially when school is in session."

Kathleen's heart leaped at the mention of school. She had worried that they didn't have a school way out here in the middle of nowhere. Aunt Elizabeth picked up one of the stovetop burners with a long iron hook and stoked the fire. "If this pail of ice will hurry up and melt, I can get some coffee perking to warm you up. You'll be needing it by the time you get done with your chores.

"Lindsay, your brothers are already out in the barn — you two had better run along. I think there is something out there that might interest you," she continued, giving her daughter a good-morning hug. A curious smile played around Aunt Elizabeth's lips. What could possibly be in the barn this early in the morning that could create so much intrigue?

"Oh, Mama, you don't mean — has — has Nelly had her foal? Is she okay?" Lindsay asked anxiously.

"Well, I'm not sure if your little mare has given you a foal yet, but last I heard she was getting pretty close to it."

Lindsay grabbed Kathleen's hand and headed toward the door. "Quick! Nelly needs us in the barn!"

"Don't forget your coats, mittens, and hats. You'll surely catch your death if you don't bundle up." Aunt Elizabeth's eyes twinkled with joy.

Lindsay's fingers trembled as she buttoned her coat.

Kathleen's heart beat wildly, and she wasn't even sure why, but she knew that if anything could make her cousin this excited it must be something big.

Lindsay grabbed a lantern and they headed out into the stillness of the dark, early morning. Kathleen shivered as a cold gust of wind whipped around the house and up under her coat. The small flame of the lantern flickered. Lindsay appeared not to notice. Her eyes were fixed on the barn. Kathleen wrapped her coat tighter around her and thought about Lindsay's remarks the night before about her dresses not being the right kind of clothes for the farm. Lindsay's overalls looked a lot warmer.

They trudged through knee-deep snow, which crunched under their feet, trying to follow a path left by bigger footsteps than theirs. Slowly, the light flickering through the crack in the barn door grew brighter. A faint whinny came from within the barn.

"I can hear her! Poor Nelly, having a foal must be awful." Lindsay broke into a run. Kathleen followed at her heels.

They burst through the large door out of breath. It was much warmer inside and it smelled of sweet hay. A cow mooed somewhere nearby. In the lantern light,

Kathleen's Unforgettable Winter

Kathleen could see Alex and Bruce talking in hushed tones outside a stall near the middle of the barn. Alex was eighteen—the oldest of all the grandchildren—but he wasn't the tallest. Bruce, his younger brother, was half a head taller than his older brother.

The girls rushed to the boys' sides and peered through gaps in the stall's railing. Lindsay gasped and Kathleen stared in amazement. A large honey-colored mare with a pure white mane rested on her side in a soft bed of hay. The horse nickered softly, picked up her head, and looked at her side where a wet little ball of fur with four lanky legs lay next to her.

"She's such a little doll!" Lindsay put her hand over her mouth and slowly knelt down to get a better look through the railings.

"Shh! She's just minutes old," Bruce whispered. He motioned the girls to stay where they were. Kathleen sank down next to Lindsay. The new mama nudged her little filly affectionately and licked its coat clean. The baby horse looked just like her mother—only she had a perfect star on her forehead and a pure white sock on her left front leg.

"It's a filly, just like you said it would be." Alex wiped his hands on a rag. "Nelly needed a little help at the end, but she's in great shape now."

"I just knew she'd have a girl!" Lindsay said quietly, as if she could not really believe it.

"Now that you've had a good look, you'd better get to your chores. Clover needs milking and those eggs

32

need to be gathered," Alex said as he picked up a pitch-fork. "The new mama and baby need to be left alone for a bit."

Lindsay stood. "Oh, I could watch her all day."

"She'll still be here when your chores are done," Bruce said as he rolled the wheelbarrow over to the stalls on the other side. They were filled with Highland cattle like the hairy creatures Kathleen had seen at the Highland Games last summer in Monroeville.

Lindsay slowly walked over to the feed bins and handed Kathleen a large soiled apron. Kathleen gingerly put it over her head and secured the ties around her waist. Lindsay filled Kathleen's apron with two big scoops of feed. All the time, she kept watching the stall where Nelly and her new little baby were. "Here, take this and go feed the chickens. When you're done, make sure to gather all the eggs."

"Hey, watch what you're doing, little sister," called Bruce. "That's not the chicken food — or were you wanting the chickens to grow wool!" Bruce laughed.

Lindsay blushed and tried not to catch her brother's eye.

Kathleen emptied her apron full of sheep food back in the bin and then Lindsay replaced it with chicken feed. Kathleen could not have told the difference, but obviously there was one.

Kathleen felt silly asking, but she had no idea how to feed the chickens or where to find the eggs.

Kathleen's Unforgettable Winter

"You've never gathered eggs before?" Lindsay looked at her like she'd just told her she didn't know how to add two plus two.

Lindsay carefully explained how. Kathleen felt so childish, as if she were a five-year-old.

She carried her precious cargo into the chicken coop. The red hens clucked and scampered toward her, anxiously awaiting their breakfast. Amongst them stood a rather large red rooster, twice the size of the other chickens. He stared at Kathleen with beady black eyes and flapped his wings at her. It was obvious he didn't want her coming inside.

"Are you sure I have to go into the pen to feed them?" Kathleen asked Alex as he walked by with a pitchfork full of hay. She did not dare take her eyes off the rooster.

"Why? Are you afraid?" Alex winked good-naturedly, but it made Kathleen feel even more foolish. "Oh, it's Big Red, isn't it? Well, all you have to do is ignore his fierce looks. He's all show and no guts."

"All show and no what?"

"No guts. You know, he acts tough, but really he's a chicken. Just act like you're confident and know what you're doing and he won't put a hurt to you."

Kathleen nodded her head as if to agree, but inside she was not so sure. What did Alex mean by 'put a hurt to her'? She noticed the sharp spurs on Big Red's legs. They looked like they'd hurt if he scratched her with them. But one thing was for sure, she didn't want Alex to think she was afraid.

A Surprise at the Farm

Alex had said, be confident. She could do that. With head held high, she strode through the door into the chicken coop and tried to steady her trembling hand as she scattered the feed around her feet. The chickens scampered to peck at the grain. As she worked, she kept one eye on Big Red, watching his every move.

"Not too bad . . . for a city girl," Alex said as he walked back by.

His comment made Kathleen more determined than ever to prove she could fit in.

"I know I have a lot to learn." Kathleen tossed another handful of feed onto the ground.

"Don't worry, it will come." Alex pitched hay into the milk cow's stall next to her.

Bruce must have overheard the conversation. "We plan to make you into a farm girl and an Annie Oakley before you return to the big city," he called from a huge draft horse's stall that he was cleaning.

"What's an 'Annie Oakley'?" Kathleen asked. Big Red spread his wings, squawked, and headed straight toward her. She dumped the rest of the contents of her apron on the ground, quickly stepped outside the coop, and shut the wire door behind her. Big Red ran as far as the feed pile, stopped, and eagerly pecked at it. Kathleen hoped that Bruce hadn't notice how frightened she was.

"You don't know who Annie Oakley was?" Bruce shook his head in disbelief.

"No. Who was she?" Kathleen swallowed. Not only was she ignorant about this person, but she still had to collect the eggs. Maybe while Big Red was busy eating she could get in and out without his noticing. She opened the gate and stepped back inside.

"Why, she was the best shot in the West!" said Bruce. "And she grew up right here in Ohio. When Annie was your age, she was such a good shot that the men in her family sent her out to do the hunting each winter. By the time she was grown, she was known far and wide for her shooting ability. She performed in all sorts of gun shows—even did some in Europe."

"Really? I've always wanted to shoot a gun. Papa keeps a pistol in his bedroom at home, but I've never been allowed to touch it." Kathleen gently patted the hay in each hen box as Lindsay had told her how to do, feeling around for the smooth brown eggs. "He says that they're dangerous if you don't know what you're doing. Someday Papa says he'll teach me how to shoot, but I guess we just haven't had the time."

"We can take care of that." Bruce climbed up the rail of the stall he was cleaning and leaned over so he could see Kathleen clearly through the chicken wire coop. "I'm going hunting in the woods along the river before the end of next week. If it's okay with your father, you can come along and be my Annie Oakley. Hopefully, we can harvest a big buck and fill our smokehouse. That would sure start off the new year on the right foot."

Was that a mischievous look in Bruce's eye? What was Bruce up to? Even though she had been five, she

could clearly remember the last trick he'd played on her. Could she trust him now?

"Aren't there wolves down by the river?" she asked, remembering Papa's story.

"Wolves? Nah, it's perfectly safe, if that's what is worrying you." Bruce jumped off the rail and scooped dung from the horses' stall next to the chicken coop and dumped it into the wheelbarrow. "But if you're too nervous . . ."

That was it. She wouldn't have him thinking she was afraid. "You ask my papa's permission. If he says yes, I'll go." Kathleen placed the last egg in her apron, took a deep breath, and prayed silently that her papa would say no. She wasn't sure if she could really trust Bruce. His hunting trip might turn out to be one of his tricks. The last place she wanted to be was tied up or left alone in the woods along the riverbank. But the thought of Bruce thinking of her as a petrified city girl outweighed all other fears.

New Life

You have made known to me the path of life;
you will fill me with joy in your presence,
with eternal pleasures at your right hand.

PSALM 16:11

Kathleen stepped out of the chicken coop and gently moved the eggs from her apron to a basket near the grain bin. She looked around trying to figure out where Lindsay was. Kathleen had been so distracted by her conversation with Bruce about hunting that she failed to notice her cousin leave.

"Lindsay? Hello? Where are you?" Kathleen peeked through the wooden slats of the cow stall where Uncle John was milking the Jersey cow.

"I'm up here! In the rafters above you." Lindsay's laugh came from somewhere overhead. She was perched on a rafter that extended out from the hayloft.

"How did you get up there?" asked Kathleen.

"I'll show you!" Lindsay jumped off the rafter and landed out of sight in a stall next to the milk cows. Dust and bits of dried grass flew into the air.

Kathleen gasped. Had Lindsay fallen? Or had she jumped on purpose? "Lindsay, are you okay?"

Lindsay climbed over the wall of the pen laughing and covered with hay. "Did I give you a scare?" she asked, brushing off her denim overalls. Pieces of hay clung to her braids.

"You aren't hurt?" Kathleen asked. The rafter looked to be about as high as her tree house at home and she would never dream of jumping out of it.

"Hurt? Not at all. I love jumping into that pile of hay! Come on, I'll show you how to get up there so you can try it."

Lindsay grabbed Kathleen's hand and led her to the ladder.

"Are you sure this is okay?"

"Sure, we do it all the time. Come on."

They climbed up into the loft. In the dim lantern light from below, Kathleen could see large piles of hay that reached clear up into the loft rafters. They walked down a narrow path between the sweet-smelling stacks that towered on both sides of them. Soon they edged their way out onto the beam that Lindsay had jumped from earlier. Kathleen's heart beat with excitement. The soft golden mound looked awfully small from where she stood.

Lindsay grabbed Kathleen's hand. "Okay, let's both jump on the count of three."

"Wait a minute! What about my dress? Lindsay! You're in overalls, but my dress will fly up over my head." Kathleen edged back toward the loft.

"Why would that matter? You might just get a little bit of straw stuck to your bloomers," Lindsay shrugged. "And I don't see how that could hurt anything."

"But Alex and Bruce are down there." By now Kathleen was safely back on the floor of the loft.

Lindsay put her hands in her pockets with a look of disappointment. "I didn't think about that." She peered over the edge and looked around the barn. "It looks like they've stepped into the tack room for a minute, so if we hurry, it won't matter one bit."

"Are you sure?"

"Yes, the door is shut, but I can hear them talking in there. Come on. It's now or never."

Kathleen was now out of excuses. She walked back out on the beam and looked down at the soft pile of hay below. It had looked rather fun. She grabbed Lindsay's hand. "Let's go!"

She jumped. The next instant Kathleen felt herself falling through the air. Then everything went dark as her heavy coat and dress flew up over her face. Kathleen could no longer see the fluffy pile of hay. Her pulse surged. What if she missed it? What if she landed on top of Lindsay? *Kawump.* Hay flew in every direction as Kathleen landed. She brushed her coat away from her face.

"Are you in there? Everything okay?" Lindsay asked, grabbing her hand and pulling her to her feet.

"I—I'm fine." Kathleen laughed. She brushed straw off her coat and out of her hair. "That was the most fun I've ever had. Next time, I'm going to hold my skirt down."

The girls jumped several more times before the boys emerged from the tack room. Then Lindsay led Kathleen through a secret tunnel in the hayloft to her hideout. The sun had finally risen and a dim light shown through the cracks in the wall. Through the filtered light, Kathleen could make out a little clearing in the back corner of the barn. It was simple with only a small apple box to sit on and a worn-out old blanket, but it reminded Kathleen of her tree house back home. She felt a twinge of homesickness. She wondered what Lucy was doing. Did Freddie miss her as he said he would?

"I don't get to come here often," Lindsay said, "but now that you are here, I'm sure we'll finish all our morning chores in half the time—like we did this morning. I've already fed the sheep, cleaned their stalls, and milked Clover. And you've fed the chickens and gathered their eggs, and we still have at least fifteen minutes before breakfast. Of course, school is starting next week, and that will put a damper on things."

"Don't you like school?" Kathleen asked.

Lindsay shrugged. "Why should I? Some people may enjoy sitting in a cold, one-room schoolhouse reading books and doing arithmetic all day, but I don't see any purpose in it. I would just as soon ride Nelly, and now that I have a new filly to train . . ."

41

Kathleen wasn't sure how to respond. She loved school and couldn't imagine wanting to miss a day. She carefully studied Lindsay's face, trying to understand what she was thinking. She knew her cousin was smart. There must be a reason she didn't like school. What could it be? "Lindsay, there is so much to learn and discover in this world. Everyone needs an education. Even if you plan to live on a farm your whole life."

"Maybe." Lindsay shrugged and looked away quickly so Kathleen could no longer read her expression.

"Are you behind? Is that it?" Papa had told Kathleen that because of the remoteness of the school, there were years, when he was a boy, that they were not able to find a teacher. "I can help you catch up. My parents gave me the most delightful literature book for Christmas. We could read it together and get a head start on the school year! It will be fun to study together." Kathleen could feel her excitement rising. She so wanted Lindsay to catch a vision for learning.

Lindsay's expression darkened. "That might work. We better get cleaned up for breakfast," she said softly, then without another word she turned and crawled back through the hay tunnel.

It was obvious Kathleen had touched a tender subject, maybe even hurt her cousin's feelings. But by the time they were back on the barn floor, Lindsay seemed to have forgotten the whole conversation.

New Life

"Do you think we should check on Nelly and her filly before we head in for breakfast?" Lindsay asked nonchalantly, pretending not to care.

Kathleen thought it rather an odd question until she noticed a twitch around the corners of Lindsay's mouth and realized that her disinterest was just a joke.

"Do I think we should? I think we must! Suppose Nelly needs more water or hay in her stall. It would simply be irresponsible for us not to check on them," Kathleen said with her hands on her hips. Both girls nodded in mock seriousness and rushed to Nelly's stall.

"As if I could have gone back to the house without first taking another look at your new little filly." Kathleen laughed.

The girls quietly approached the stall and gazed at the newborn filly who was trying its hardest to stand up on its long, shaky legs. Nelly nickered softly and gently nudged her little one. Finally, the filly stood and took a few wobbly steps toward its mother's side and began to nurse.

"She's so precious," Kathleen whispered as she climbed down the rail. "What are you going to name her?"

"I'm not sure yet," Lindsay said. "Maybe I'll think of something by the time we finish the house chores."

Kathleen looked at Lindsay. House chores? One thing she could tell already about living on the farm — work was never done.

Kathleen's Unforgettable Winter

Kathleen could not wait to go back to the barn and check on Nelly and the new filly. But it was wash day. Washing clothes with a scrub board and wringing them out by hand instead of using the automatic machines they had at home took a lot more time and energy.

Grandma Maggie showed Kathleen how. "Rub the shirt with a bit of soap," she said with her strong Scottish accent. "Mind that you get just enough and do not waste. Then, you scrub up and down the washboard like this." Kathleen could see that Grandma Maggie's strong arms were accustomed to such hard work. She looked at the large load of laundry piled on the kitchen table and wondered if they would ever finish.

Grandma Maggie smiled. "I know it looks like a lot, lass, but we have three scrub boards, and between your aunt, your mama, Lindsay, and you, we'll be done in no time." She handed Kathleen a pair of wool socks. "Here, lassie, you try your hand at it."

Kathleen, Lindsay, and Aunt Elizabeth scrubbed while Grandma and Mama rinsed, wrung out the water, and hung the clothes up to dry on a makeshift clothesline stretched across the living room.

After lunch Grandma Maggie solicited Richard and Robby's help in rinsing the clothes so she could make her famous sugar cookies.

"There's nothing like the smell of your sugar cookies to make us motivated to finish early." Lindsay scrubbed a little harder.

44

New Life

It was afternoon when the last of the laundry was hung up to dry. They all sat around the kitchen table and munched on warm sugar cookies and cold milk. Grandma's sugar cookies were as good as Kathleen remembered. But as much as she liked them, Kathleen could not wait to go back to the barn to see the new filly.

Finally, when all their housework was done, the girls bundled back up in their heavy winter coats and raced back to the barn.

Kathleen followed Lindsay's example and climbed up on the stall to get a better look at the newborn. They dangled their arms over the top rail and both girls stood quietly admiring the beautiful new filly. Kathleen smiled as Nelly gently nuzzled her baby and nickered affectionately.

Kathleen never dreamed she'd see a baby horse just minutes after its birth. She had heard people talk about the miracle of new life and now she understood what they meant—to think that just hours ago that filly was inside Nelly and now she was here, breathing the same air as she was. Kathleen could not wait to write Lucy and tell her all about Nelly and her new baby.

"How long have you owned Nelly?" Kathleen asked after silently watching the mare and her filly for some time. She loved to watch the filly's soft brown eyes as it curiously studied its new world.

"Just over a year. Pa surprised me with her for my thirteenth birthday. I couldn't believe she was really mine. For as long as I can remember I had always wanted a horse,"

Lindsay said. Nelly wandered near enough that Lindsay reached out and tenderly stroked her on the nose.

Kathleen thought of her birthday and the way she felt when Papa and Richard had made the tree house for her. A sharp pain pierced her heart. She missed home miserably—and Lucy. She ached to see her friend. Had it only been one week? How was she going to manage? Taking a deep breath, Kathleen silently voiced her heart to the Lord.

Dear Jesus, please keep Lucy safe and healthy while I am gone. And Lord, she misses her brother Peter so much—could You please allow him to move home? Lucy says he wants to become a doctor someday and that he cannot attend school right now. Lucy says Peter is forced to study on his own because the responsibilities on his grandparents' farm are so great.

When Kathleen finished her prayer, it occurred to her that she was in a similar situation as Lucy's brother. Now that she missed Lucy, she understood how much Peter and Lucy must miss each other. For some unexplainable reason, Kathleen felt burdened to pray for him like she did for Lucy, almost as if she loved him just as much. After all, she really did kind of know him— Lucy had talked about him so much.

"Kathleen, why the sad look on your face? Do you not like the name Doll for Nelly's filly?" Lindsay looked slightly offended.

"Doll?" Kathleen realized Lindsay must have been talking to her while she'd been deep in thought and she hadn't heard her. "Why no, it is not that at all. I just—"

"Do you have a better idea?" Lindsay asked.

"Oh dear, I'm sorry. I was thinking about something totally different. But now that you ask, Doll is nice, but let me think . . . I know! What if you name her Dream? You said it was always your dream to own a horse of your own, and now you have two horses."

"Dream? That seems kind of silly. I don't know if I've ever daydreamed about anything." Lindsay's eyes widened, and her face showed that Kathleen's idea was foolish. "I guess there's no harm in it, but it just seems to me that having a dream is just setting yourself up for disappointment." Lindsay shrugged, dismissing Kathleen's suggestion entirely.

Kathleen was about to defend herself, but she realized it was useless. Lindsay wouldn't understand. They were opposites. But oddly their differences intrigued her. She hoped she would grow to love Lindsay—even though half the time she hardly understood her. So far she'd learned that Lindsay was kind, cared about the animals, worked hard, and was practical and down-to-earth.

"You're right. Dream would not be a suitable name for your horse." Kathleen looked at the filly's sweet face with the perfect tiny star on its forehead and the solid white sock on her left front leg. "Doll is the best name. After all, it really does fit her."

"Then Doll it will be!" Lindsay said with a satisfied grin.

Kathleen smiled too, but Lindsay's words about the dangers of dreaming set her to thinking. Could dreaming

be bad? Surely not! There was no harm in it, unless of course you set your heart too intently on a certain outcome. There could be nothing wrong with hoping for great things. Dreaming about winning the State Spelling Bee had turned out for good. Where would this world be if there were no dreamers? Some of the greatest inventions started with a simple dream. Like the telephone and the radio.

Kathleen sighed heavily. She knew that deep down she was not thinking about dreaming in general; she was thinking about the National Spelling Bee. She had not lost hope that somehow, someway, she would still be able to go to Washington, D.C.

Was it too much to hope for? Was she setting herself up for disappointment?

4

Hunting in Wolf Territory

*Consider it pure joy, my brothers, whenever you face trials
of many kinds, because you know that the testing
of your faith develops perseverance.*

JAMES 1:2–3

Kathleen had hoped Bruce would forget about his offer to take her hunting, but he held true to his pledge and asked her papa's permission. Papa said yes, and Bruce made plans for a trip at the beginning of the next week. Kathleen tried to assure herself that if her papa trusted Bruce, then she could. However, with each passing day the uneasy feeling she had in her stomach grew.

In the long winter evenings, Kathleen tried to distract her fearful worries about the hunt by reading *Ben-Hur* to Lindsay by candlelight. It was during one of these sessions that she realized Lindsay could hardly read. No wonder she didn't like school. Kathleen was determined to help Lindsay improve her reading skills.

Kathleen's Unforgettable Winter

During the day, she tried to stuff her anxieties deep within her heart and focus all her energies on learning the varying chores that farm life demanded. Lindsay and she spent most of the day going from house chores, to barn chores, and back to the house again. Even then, Kathleen still had an uneasy feeling whenever she thought of Bruce. The only time she was totally able to forget her dread of Bruce's pranks and her fear of man-eating wolves was during her frequent visits with Lindsay to see Nelly's new filly.

Just as Lucy had suggested, Kathleen was enjoying the adventures of life on a farm and she spent time every day writing Lucy to tell her all about it. There were some things she missed about life in the city, like listening to her favorite radio shows and having indoor plumbing. Most of all she missed spending the evenings with her parents. They ate together at mealtimes and they worked together throughout the day, but at night they were in different houses. She missed her papa's calling out her spelling words each evening and being able to slip out of bed at night to talk to her mama whenever anything was weighing on her heart, like the upcoming hunt and how she missed Lucy and school and how often she didn't feel like she fit in at the farm. Even though she tried as hard as she could, Kathleen still felt like a clumsy city girl. She had so much to learn about farm life.

Kathleen also missed their family devotions and her mother's playing the piano, as well as her papa's reading from the Scriptures. Grandpa McKenzie would

read to everyone from the large family Bible each morning directly after breakfast. But it wasn't the same. Kathleen missed having devotions and talking and sharing with her immediate family. Unfortunately, there didn't seem to be any time for that on the farm. Everyone had to work so hard. Now she understood why her grandpa and grandma and aunt and uncle had never been to visit them in Fort Wayne.

The night before the hunt, Kathleen could not sleep. She longed to talk to someone and express her thoughts and concerns.

Jumping out of bed, she fumbled around in the dark until she found a match and lit the candle that sat on her nightstand. Kathleen tiptoed quietly, so she would not wake Lindsay, to the large trunk in the corner of the room. Besides her clothes, and the few items she had placed around Lindsay's room, it held all her precious belongings that she brought from Fort Wayne. She grabbed a pen and paper, settled herself on the floor, and began to compose a letter to Lucy. She spilled her heart out, sharing things that she knew Lindsay would not understand—how busy life had been her first week on the farm, the adjustments that she faced, and how she was trying her hardest to fit in, though she felt awkward most of the time. Finally, she expressed to Lucy the apprehensions she felt about the next day's adventures:

Perhaps I am allowing my imagination to get the better of me, but I fear that this hunting trip tomorrow might

prove to be extremely perilous — that my very life is at stake. And just in case this is true . . . in case we never see each other in this world again, I want you to know that you have been a most wonderful friend, and I'm sure I will miss you — even in heaven. I love you ever so dearly.
> *Forever friends,*
> *Kathleen*
> *P.S. You can have my tree house.*

As she hid the letter deep within her trunk, Kathleen wondered if she'd gotten carried away. But by the time she blew out the candle and snuggled under her blankets, she had convinced herself that she had made the right decision. If she died, Lucy would be glad she had written her a letter, and if she returned safely, she could cut out that section of the note and no one would ever know.

The next afternoon Kathleen finished churning the butter, the last of her chores for the day, and settled down on the rug in front of the living room fireplace to practice her spelling words. Robby and Richard sat nearby playing jacks.

"I won," said Richard.

"Here, let me go first this time." Robby reached for the ball in Richard's hand.

"Didn't you go first last time?" Richard held the ball back.

"No, you did."

"That was the time before. You did go first last time, I remember," Richard said.

"Boys, don't quarrel," said Kathleen. "Why don't you let the loser go first?"

"That's a great idea," said Robby. Richard frowned at her but then agreed to the compromise, and they dumped the jacks on the floor between them and started playing once again.

Kathleen smiled — she missed Richard. She hardly ever saw him these days except at mealtime. The farm was big and they both were kept busy with chores. And when Richard wasn't helping out, he and Robby were off exploring.

She looked down at her book. 'Promenade', she read. She looked up and silently spelled it to herself, p-r-o-m-e-n-a-d-e. Checking the written word, she was sure she'd spelled it right. 'Prominence' was next on her list. P-r-o-m-i-n-e-n-c-e. She looked. Correct.

Just then Bruce walked into the room. "There you are. I've been looking all over for you. It's time for our hunting trip."

"Can I go?" asked Robby and Richard in unison, as they leaped up from the floor and looked eagerly at Bruce.

Bruce wrestled them back down to the floor in a playful way. "Not this time, fellers. Maybe when you get a little older."

"Aw, shucks," said Robby, returning to the game of jacks.

Kathleen's Unforgettable Winter

Kathleen had been dreading this moment. She had an idea. "I'm not sure I can go, Bruce. I think your mother needs me to help with dinner."

"I already talked with her and she says you're released from your duties. But we have to hurry. There's only a few hours left before dark." He stood up.

Kathleen put her spelling book down.

"You're not backing out on me, are you?" A smile played at the corner of Bruce's mouth.

"No, of course not," Kathleen said.

"Dress warm. It gets awfully cold out there."

Kathleen shivered as she thought of how cold she had been since she arrived at the farm.

Surprisingly enough, she was colder at night and in the morning in the house than when she was working outside or in the barn. The only thing Kathleen could attribute that to was the fact she was working all day long.

"Will my wool dress, stockings, and my thick coat keep me warm enough?"

"Hardly. A dress will never do. Don't you have wool pants?"

"Pants? I've never worn pants in my life," Kathleen said indignantly, trying to imagine what Madelyn or Patricia would say if they ever saw her in pants.

"Never worn pants? How do you run those foot races your papa says you are so fast at?" Bruce asked in surprise.

"Oh! That's different. I have knickers designed especially for our track team. They're much shorter than

pants, and they're just for wearing when I'm running." Kathleen was glad Lindsay was out in the barn looking after Nelly and her new baby. She didn't want her to overhear what she'd just said. Overalls were obviously Lindsay's favorite thing to wear. And even though Kathleen could not imagine herself wearing men's clothing, she thought her cousin looked oddly cute in them.

Bruce chuckled. "My sister doesn't seem to mind wearing Alex's and my hand-me-down overalls. Go have Lindsay fetch you a pair." He started to leave.

"Are you serious?" She wanted to say something about never being seen in men's pants, but Bruce stopped and the look in his eyes stopped her.

"Dead serious. I haven't ever lost a hunting partner and I don't plan to have one freeze to death on this trip either."

"Well—okay, if I must. I'll go ask Lindsay if I can borrow a pair of hers. I suppose no one will see us . . . will they?" Kathleen blushed at the thought of being seen in men's pants.

"Of course not. The only living things that will see us are the deer and wolves we're hunting. And the pants will come in handy if we have to run and escape for our lives."

"Wolves?" Kathleen knew he was kidding; she could see it in his eyes, but the thought of seeing a wolf made her cringe.

"Don't worry, Kathleen," said Robby, getting up from the floor where he and Richard were still playing

jacks. "Bruce likes to tell scary stories. It used to scare me when I was little, but Pa told me that his stories about wolves and stuff are not true—not even a little bit true. Pa says that there really were wolves when Grandpa was a boy, but that was years and years ago."

"Thanks, Robby." Kathleen tousled his curly red hair and tried not to laugh at his reference to when he was young, as if seven years old was all grown up.

"You'd better hurry," said Bruce. "We're running out of daylight."

Kathleen grabbed her coat and rushed out to the barn to ask Lindsay if she could borrow a pair of her pants.

She found Lindsay brushing Nelly. "The only ones I have are hand-me-downs from Bruce and Alex. But you're welcome to try them. They are in the bottom drawer of my dresser. You'll probably need to tie them up around your waist with a rope to keep them on, though," Lindsay said. She went into the tack room and found a piece of rope that was hanging on the wall. She handed it to Kathleen.

Kathleen ran up the stairs to their room. Lindsay did not have many clothes, so it was not hard for Kathleen to find what Lindsay was talking about. She cinched the patched, brown wool pants around her small waist and pulled several layers of faded green sweaters over her head. The best way to describe the form that looked back at her in the mirror was the big stuffed scarecrow that she had seen in the barn. When Kathleen asked why they had an overstuffed "hay man" in the barn,

Lindsay had explained that their scarecrow, whom they affectionately called Mr. Smith, did a brilliant job of scaring away birds and rabbits from the garden during the growing season.

"He's a cold-blooded sort of man, so we have to bring him in during the winter," Lindsay teased. "Bruce recommended that we name him Mr. Johnston, after our cold-hearted neighbor—he's the grouchiest man in the county. But Grandpa and Pa wouldn't hear of it. They say that we should spend our energy praying for our neighbor, not making fun of him. So Mr. Smith it is."

Kathleen gazed at her reflection in the full-length mirror. "Well, you can call me Miss Smith." All she needed was a little straw sticking out of her here and there. She laughed aloud, and then her face sobered.

Did scarecrows frighten away wolves as well as they did birds and rabbits? Wait a minute, Robby had said Bruce was telling a story to frighten her and that there were no wolves. There she was letting her imagination run away with her again. Kathleen took a deep breath.

She straightened her shoulders. No matter what, she was determined to go. She would not let her cousin Bruce think that she was a prissy city girl.

"How do I look?" Kathleen asked her mama and grandpa as she bounded through the kitchen.

"Good and warm, lass. Good and warm." Grandpa took a sip of coffee. "You'll be needing every bit of that warmth when the sun goes down."

Mama set her coffee cup down on the table and stood up. "Do be careful," she said as she gave Kathleen a long hug.

Grandpa must've seen the fear in Mama's eyes, for he said, "Don't fret your mind a bit, Claire. Bruce is a responsible lad to be sure."

"I'll be careful, Mama, I promise." Kathleen slipped her coat on and rushed out the door.

Bruce was waiting for her by the woodpile. When he spied her, he smiled approvingly. "That's more like it." He handed her a large rifle.

"You might make an Annie Oakley yet. Let's see how you handle my 30-30 Winchester Rifle. I've placed an empty tin can on the fence post over yonder." He pointed to a small can that stood on the wooden fence that separated the field from the backyard.

The target looked pretty small to Kathleen. "Can we get closer?"

"There's nothing to it — just lift up the barrel, line up the sights, slowly pull the trigger, and let the gun do all the work." Bruce helped Kathleen position the butt of the gun against her shoulder and showed her how to line the sight up with the bead at the end of the gun.

"Is that all you have to do?" Kathleen asked.

"Sure is. But hitting the target might be harder than you expect. Don't be discouraged if — "

"Can I shoot now?" Kathleen said. "This isn't as complicated as I thought it would be." She held the gun steady against her shoulder.

"Whenever you're ready. Just don't expect to hit the target the—"

Bang! The gun rang out and almost instantly the tin can flew into the air.

"You did it! You actually hit the can!" Bruce stood with his mouth wide open, a look of amazement written across his face. He obviously was so shocked that Kathleen burst into laughter.

"Let's go hunting." Kathleen handed Bruce the gun and started walking toward the wooded riverbank.

"Where—where are you going?" Bruce managed to get out.

"Hunting. Aren't you coming?" Kathleen asked with a confident smile. She knew that if there had been any doubt in Bruce's mind as to whether or not she could make it in the country, there wasn't any more. She felt that she had sufficiently proven herself to him and finally won his respect.

After that Bruce's whole attitude changed toward Kathleen. On the way to their hunting spot, he explained to Kathleen all about the deer and what to expect in their behavior. He no longer treated her like his dainty little cousin from the city that he liked to tease. He seemed to take her more seriously and treat her with respect.

"Most of the time, they won't come out until right before dark. We want to get in position early so we

don't startle them. They have keen eyesight and hearing. I've made a little shelter out of dead tree branches and the like, but even with that you'll have to sit as still and quiet as a frozen mouse."

The snowdrifts were incredibly deep in some places and walking was hard work. Kathleen was toasty warm by the time they reached Bruce's makeshift hunting shelter overlooking the river. But five minutes after she sat on the frozen ground inside the crude three-sided fortress, the biting wind worked its way through her layers and she was cold.

"You look out this way toward the river." Bruce pointed through a small opening in between the branches. "I'll watch behind us, back toward the field."

"All right." Kathleen shivered. The sky was overcast, making the late afternoon air seem even colder. She shifted positions, trying to stay warm.

A few moments later, Kathleen spied a dark shadow moving through the edge of the wooded area on the opposite riverbank. She held her breath. As she watched, the figure moved silently through the trees. Her heart pounded in her ears. A tan-colored shoulder appeared through a break in the trees, followed by a long body and white tail.

She pointed at the figure. "Bruce," she whispered, but it was too late. Whatever it was had disappeared.

"What did you see?"

"I'm not sure, but it was big, and it was walking in the trees along the bank. I think you should get your

gun ready," Kathleen said, keeping her eyes on where she last saw the animal.

Bruce crawled over on his belly and settled himself beside her. His gun tucked tight against his shoulder.

"There it is again!" Kathleen pointed. "Near the riverbank."

"Where? What is it?" Bruce propped himself up on his elbows to get a better view. Now the animal was fully exposed and Kathleen could see it clearly.

"It's a deer—a huge one at that!" In her excitement Kathleen's voice rose a little more than it should have. The buck stopped, threw its head up, and looked straight at her. Kathleen froze.

Dear Lord, please don't let me scare it away.

The huge buck stood unmoving like a regal statue, his heavy horns glinting in the sunlight like a crown. Kathleen looked at the sharp points on his rack and a new thought entered her head.

Were deer dangerous? He wasn't that far away and what if he decided to charge?

Just then the buck stomped his foot against the ground and hot steam blew from his nostrils. Kathleen wanted to run, but she forced herself to stay still.

What was Bruce doing? That animal looked like it was going to charge them.

The buck stomped again, then turned back toward the woods. Kathleen sighed.

A shot rang out next to her.

Kathleen's Unforgettable Winter

Startled, she jumped. The buck flinched and with one quick bound disappeared into the dark shade of the forest. Kathleen was relieved that the huge buck with the menacing horns had run away from them instead of toward them.

Bruce leaped to his feet. "I hit him! I know I did." He reloaded the gun.

"You did? How can you tell?" Kathleen's heart surged with excitement.

"Did you notice him lurch before he jumped into the woods? I'm pretty sure I hit him soundly. We sure could use the meat. He was an unusually large deer—it would be a crime to lose him."

"What now?" Kathleen asked.

"We'll have to track his blood trail, but first, we must wait. If we push him, he'll get up and run much further. I think it best to give him at least thirty minutes," Bruce whispered, his eyes fixed on the last place they had seen the buck.

The next half hour dragged on forever. Kathleen tried her hardest to sit still, but she was so curious to see what happened to the buck that she found herself fidgeting with the buttons on her coat, twisting and twirling her hair, or subconsciously snapping twigs from the dead branches that formed their little shelter. Finally, Bruce bent over and told her it was time to go.

"Kathleen, you stay here while I follow his trail," Bruce whispered.

"Stay here? By myself? I'm too scar—what I mean is that, I would sure love to track that deer with you."

"I know you want to help, but I've thought it through. We desperately need that meat and if I take you back to the house, it'll be too dark to track him. And by morning, the trail may be lost with a new snowfall. I'd take you with me, but the terrain is too rough and the snow too deep. I shouldn't be gone long. You'll be safe here."

"Okay," Kathleen said quietly, trying to sound more confident than she felt. "But I really do want to go with you."

"Thanks, Kathleen. You're a real trooper. I'll leave the gun with you—just in case you need it for any reason. I have my trusty knife." Bruce patted the long knife sheath that hung from his belt with one hand and handed Kathleen the gun with the other.

"How long will you be?" Kathleen asked.

"A half hour at the most. I'll be back before dark. Just wait here." Bruce rose and walked briskly away through the snow.

Kathleen watched until he disappeared into the woods in the same place she had last seen the deer. Then she listened to the snow crunching beneath the weight of his boots until the sound faded from her ears. Kathleen tried to convince herself that all would be well, but her heart beat so fast that she could feel it throbbing in her temples. The minutes dragged by and soon Kathleen was convinced that Bruce had been gone much longer than the thirty minutes he predicted.

Alone in the Woods

*Do not fear, for I am with you; do not be dismayed,
for I am your God. I will strengthen you and help you;
I will uphold you with my righteous right hand.*

ISAIAH 41:10

Kathleen tirelessly peered out the openings of the gun shelter, searching the edge of the woods. She didn't like the feeling of being all alone and wished Bruce would return soon. Nothing escaped her notice, whether it was the swish of a fluffy squirrel's tail or the fluttering wing of a chickadee as it flitted from branch to branch feasting on winterberries. Kathleen shuddered at the creak of the trees as they swayed in the cold wind that blew through the wooded area along the river.

It grew darker as dusk neared and still no sign of Bruce. Kathleen wasn't sure if her imagination made things appear worse than they were, but she was almost positive the wind was getting stronger. She wrapped

Alone in the Woods

her coat tighter around her and sat on her hands to keep them warm. She had often imagined what it would be like to be a damsel in distress and now she was afraid that she might find out.

Something moved along the riverbank. Was it Bruce? No, it couldn't be. He'd gone the opposite way. Her heart pounded in her ears. It couldn't be any other human being either—it was too low to the ground.

What could it be? Wolves? She thought of how they used to ravage the countryside when Grandpa was young. She slid to her stomach and positioned the gun against her shoulder and pointed the barrel in the direction she'd last spotted the ominous shadow.

After several long seconds, Kathleen saw it again. This time it was closer, and she could see it clearly. It was the size of a large dog and it was black, gray, and tan—a wolf. She was positive. And it was trotting right toward her, its head low to the ground as if it was searching for her scent. Kathleen felt numb. It was stalking her. The beast was at least a hundred yards away, but Kathleen knew her time was short. Something must be done. She steadied her shaking hands, raised the butt of the gun to her shoulder, and looked down the barrel.

Kathleen searched frantically for the wolf. Each time she lined up the menacing-looking creature in the gun's sights, her heavy breathing sent the barrel high above and then below the target. The wolf appeared to have definitely picked up her scent and was now coming straight toward her at a fast trot.

65

Kathleen's Unforgettable Winter

Kathleen remembered what Bruce had said, "Take a deep breath, slowly let all the air out, hold your breath as you steady the sights, and then shoot."

She forced herself to go through each step. She held her breath and was able to steady the gun just for a second. Shutting her eyes, Kathleen pulled the trigger.

The gun resounded in her ear. Then almost immediately came a muffled yelp from the direction of the wolf.

Sitting up, she searched the ground where she'd last seen the ferocious animal. Kathleen shivered. The wind whipped her hair about her face. Darkness was closing in around her, but all appeared still along the riverbank. Nothing moved in the white snow. It was as if the predator had vanished—like it had all been a bad dream.

Kathleen slowly stood and peered over the pile of branches that made up the shelter. Her legs felt like jelly beneath her. She tried to steady her shaking hand as she secured the gun and attempted to reload.

"Nice shot!"

A voice from behind startled her. Kathleen spun around. She stood face-to-face with her cousin Alex.

"Wh-where did you c-come fr—I think I m-missed it," Kathleen stammered.

"I heard your shot, and it was definitely a hit—you can tell by the way it sounds, you know. What did you kill anyway?" Alex scanned the riverbank as he spoke.

"I—I think it was a w-wolf. A rather ferocious—big wolf." Kathleen shuddered at the memory.

Alex looked at her incredulously. "I doubt it was a wolf. You probably shot a coyote. They're a real menace to the livestock." He patted her shoulder. "Great work." He pointed at a spot. "There it is. I can see it lying over there on the ground—wow, that must have been at least a one-hundred-yard shot."

Kathleen stared at the dark spot in the snow. "Coyote? I thought for sure it was a wolf."

"Where did you get an idea like that? There haven't been any wolves in these parts for years." Alex looked at her more closely. His expression changed suddenly, and a concerned look came over his brow. "Say, where's Bruce? He should know better than to leave you alone and let you get scared like this."

"I wasn't really scared—well, maybe I was."

Alex picked up one of her hands. It was shaking badly. "I can see that." A smile spread across his face. "So, where is Bruce?"

Kathleen heard an urgency in his voice. Had something bad happened to someone back at the farm? "Is something wrong?"

Alex glanced around at the trees and down toward the river. "Grandpa says there is a doozy of a snowstorm coming. He has a way of sensing these sorts of things, and he's almost always right. I came to fetch the two of you and tell you to head for home immediately. I'd barely left the house when I noticed the winds picking up from the north and the clouds building high in the sky."

Kathleen's Unforgettable Winter

That explained why it had gotten dark so quickly and why she'd thought Bruce had been gone so long.

"Bruce shot a big buck, and it ran into the woods over there beyond the riverbank." Kathleen pointed to the opposite side of the frozen river.

"How long has he been gone?" Alex asked.

Kathleen could see the worry on her cousin's face. Light snow began to swirl about them. Grandpa must be right about the storm. It had already started.

"Kathleen, I hate to ask, but do you think you can remember how to get home by yourself?"

Kathleen shivered at the thought of being alone once again, but she knew Alex wouldn't ask her to do this if he didn't think it was safe. Still, she wasn't sure if she could find the way. "Walk home, by myself?" She looked in the direction of the farm.

"It's not that far. Just follow the tracks—they're real clear in the snow. That's how I found you."

"Okay," Kathleen nodded. She was glad Alex trusted her and she didn't want to let him down.

"Good. Go straight home and don't stop for any reason—Grandpa says this could turn into a full-blown blizzard. I'll take the gun. It will just slow you down."

"What about Bruce and the deer? And my coyote . . . what am I to do with that?" Kathleen asked.

"Don't worry about them. I have to find Bruce and warn him about the storm before it's too late. If I have time, I'll grab your coyote on the way back," Alex called over his shoulder as he ran down the riverbank.

Kathleen headed for the farmhouse, relying on the footprints Alex, Bruce, and she had left earlier to lead her home. The icy wind came in gusts now, whipping loose strands of hair around her face until it stung as if it were cutting into her flesh. Little snow flurries danced hurriedly about, and the sky above darkened to a dismal gray. Despite the deep drifts, Kathleen pressed forward as fast as she could—half running, half stumbling.

She was grateful Bruce talked her into wearing pants—she would be half frozen if she were wearing her skirt. It was cold enough with the overalls.

The snow fell harder and began to fill the footprints. Suddenly she remembered Papa's words from last summer about running the race of life. It was almost as if he was whispering in her ear. "Sometimes the path may be dark . . . but God is always there; all you need to do is call on Him."

"Dear Lord, please help me to find my way home," she prayed aloud between deep breaths. Kathleen was so frightened she could think of nothing else to pray, so she repeated the same words over and over, pleading with the Lord to guide her. Finally, she reached the edge of the woods along the river and stumbled up a small hill.

Had they gone down this hill? She couldn't remember.

Kathleen was out of breath by the time she reached the top of the hill. The air was so cold it hurt her lungs when she breathed. She squinted to protect her eyes from the thick falling snow that pelted her face.

Kathleen's Unforgettable Winter

Kathleen pushed forward even though she began to feel more and more disoriented in the swirling world that held her in its icy grip.

In the distance she saw a light flickering through the white world that enveloped her. Her heart surged with hope. "Thank You, Lord, for showing me the way, and please give me the strength to make it through this storm." Kathleen stumbled toward the light.

It wasn't until she reached the back porch of her uncle's house that Kathleen realized just how cold she had become. Now that she was safe, she noticed her teeth were chattering and her fingers and toes were numb. The wind caught the door as she pushed on the latch. It flung open and launched her shaking body into the kitchen.

The rest of the family, who had gathered around the kitchen anxiously watching and waiting for their arrival, turned as one and stared at her as if not believing their eyes. Then everyone moved at once.

Mama rushed forward and grabbed Kathleen's arm and led her shivering daughter toward the warm stove. "Thank heaven, you're home safely! You must be frozen."

Papa met her at the stove and put his strong arm around Kathleen and warmed her in his embrace. He did not need to say a word; she knew he was thanking the Lord that she was safely home.

Aunt Elizabeth looked out into the storm and when she realized that Kathleen was alone, she shut the door.

Her face looked anxious. "Where are the boys? Didn't they come with you?"

"They—they're st-still looking for the d-deer," Kathleen managed to say through her shivers. Aunt Elizabeth took one more nervous glance at the door, then rushed to the stove to put water on to boil.

"Lindsay," Aunt Elizabeth said as she grabbed the kettle off the stove and began filling it with water, "run upstairs and get some dry socks for Kathleen."

"Yes, Mama." Lindsay turned and Kathleen heard her footsteps pounding on the stairs.

"I'll have some hot tea to warm your insides in no time." Aunt Elizabeth put the kettle on a burner. "Thank heaven you made it safely. The boys grew up here and know their way around like the back of their hands, but you, Kathleen—however did you find your way through this storm? Those boys should never have left you by yourself. What were they thinking?"

Kathleen could tell that her aunt was truly relieved that she had made it safely, but she could also hear concern in her voice. Aunt Elizabeth stoked the stove fire in an obvious effort to hide her growing anxiety about her two oldest sons.

"There was a trail . . . footprints in the snow . . . Alex needed to find B-Bruce."

"Where is Bruce? Why wasn't he with you?" Uncle John clearly was just as worried as Aunt Elizabeth.

"Let the girl warm herself," said Grandma. "Then we'll get our answers."

Kathleen's Unforgettable Winter

Mama took off Kathleen's boots, revealing red toes. "I don't think they're frostbitten," said papa, "But I'm afraid they'll sting as they warm up." Mama took off her shawl and wrapped Kathleen's toes. Kathleen thought she saw tears in her mama's eyes. She wanted to tell her that she was okay, but she couldn't find the words. She was too cold.

Robby and Richard peppered her with questions, until Aunt Elizabeth made them go into the next room to play a game.

Lindsay brought her a pair of wool socks and sat in the chair next to her. "I should have gone with you. I could've shown you the way home."

It took a cup of tea, a warm blanket around her shoulders, and several minutes in front of the kitchen stove before Kathleen's teeth stopped chattering and she was warm enough to talk. As soon as she was, everyone gathered around the breakfast table next to the stove to hear Kathleen's hunting story.

Uncle John was most curious to know the exact location of where they had been hunting and seemed anxious when Kathleen could only give him a vague description. Judging from his frequent glances toward the door, Kathleen was sure that he was thinking he might have to go out in the storm and search for Alex and Bruce. "I'm sure they'll be along in a few minutes," he said. "They've been walking those woods since they were toddlers." His voice didn't sound very convincing.

Kathleen felt her fear for Alex and Bruce rising as the minutes passed.

Dear God, please bring my cousins safely home.

"Kathleen." Robby shook her arm. "Did you see any other animals while you were waiting for Bruce to find his deer?" Robby leaned his elbows on the table.

Richard's eyes were round with excitement. "What was hunting like? Did you get to shoot the gun?"

Kathleen blushed deeply. She wanted to skip the part of the story where she shot the coyote thinking it was a wolf, but she knew straightforward honesty was the only way to go. Kathleen tousled Robby's hair and smiled awkwardly.

"Yes, I shot something."

"You did! Wow, what was it?" asked Richard. "A bear? A wolf?"

Kathleen looked up at her papa, hoping he'd understand how she could make a mistake like this. After all, she had never gone hunting before. "I thought it was a wolf, but Alex said it was only a large coyote."

"You shot a coyote? That's wonderful!" exclaimed Uncle John. "Those sneaky scavengers have put a hurt on the lamb crop each year, and it hasn't been getting any better either."

She was wondering what he meant when they heard the thud of boots on the back porch. Aunt Elizabeth leaped to her feet, tripping over the kitchen stool in her effort to reach the door.

Kathleen's Unforgettable Winter

It swung open, letting in a burst of wind and snow. Alex and Bruce strode through the entrance. Kathleen immediately noticed a look of concern on the two young men's faces. Alex wasn't wearing his coat. Instead, it was wrapped around something he was carrying in his arms.

"Alex, for gracious sakes!" said Aunt Elizabeth. "Why aren't you wearing your coat? You could have frozen to death in that cold."

Alex glanced at Kathleen with a compassionate expression she could not quite figure out. Then he looked at his mama.

"I came across our neighbor's German shepherd—"

"You mean Mr. Johnston's watchdog, Bruiser!" said Robby, backing away. "That hateful ol' dog chases our wagon every time we go to town. He bit me once, you know." Robby's eyes shone with fear. It was obvious that he dreaded the dog.

"Yes, this is Old Bruiser all right." Alex gently laid his bundle on the kitchen table and unwrapped the dog from the depths of his large coat.

"You mean to tell me that's Old Bruiser—" Robby's eyes grew wide when he saw the wounded dog stretched out across the table.

Kathleen caught her breath. Something about the poor dog looked awfully familiar.

"What happened to him?" asked Lindsay.

"Is he still alive?" Uncle John rubbed his beard. "I've never seen him so calm in all my life." He leaned

74

over the dog and looked more closely at his bloodied shoulder.

"I suppose he was out hunting and evidently got himself wounded pretty badly. But I can't imagine what would put a big dog like him down." Grandpa came over and examined the wound too.

The awful truth slowly dawned on Kathleen. She hoped that her fears were not grounded, but when Uncle John gave his adamant opinion concerning the nature of the injury, Kathleen felt a sharp stab at her heart and her stomach began to feel uneasy.

"It is most definitely a bullet wound. Looks like it penetrated pretty deep in his left shoulder. We'll need to remove the bullet immediately if this dog's going to make it. Elizabeth," Uncle John said as he rolled up his sleeves, "clear the kitchen of people and make the table ready for surgery." Uncle John, usually a laid-back, cheerful sort of man, was now all business.

Aunt Elizabeth motioned for the children to leave the kitchen. They all left immediately in an excited flurry, except for Kathleen, who hung her head and slowly made her way up the dark stairway to the cold bedroom.

"What have I done?" Kathleen whispered in the dark.

Dear Lord, please help my uncle and aunt save this poor dog's life. He may have been a mean watchdog, but I'm sure his master loves him. Dear Lord, I don't want to be the cause of his tragic death.

Kathleen's Unforgettable Winter

Suddenly the struggles of the past weeks hit her — Papa losing his job, her disappointing Christmas, saying good-bye to Lucy and her other friends back home, adjusting to a new way of life, and her frightful hunt that now had turned into such a disaster. Hot tears spilled down her cheeks. She threw herself on the bed and sobbed. Kathleen could never remember feeling as weary, cold, alone, and awkward as she felt at that moment. She had tried so hard to prove to her cousin Bruce that she was not a silly city girl, and now she had done the worst possible thing she could imagine.

She wanted to go home. How could she ever face her cousins? She had tried so hard to fit in. She had thought she could, but now she knew she did not belong here.

Kathleen buried herself beneath the mound of quilts that lay across the bed and cried herself to sleep.

A Doozy of a Storm

Be joyful in hope, patient in affliction, faithful in prayer.
ROMANS 12:12

"Kathleen! Kathleen! Wake up!" Kathleen could barely see her brother through the dim morning light. Robby and he were standing over her bed. "Old Bruiser had to have surgery last night. He's recovering in the pantry, but we're not allowed to visit him."

Kathleen's pulse quickened as she remembered last night's events. She propped herself up on her elbow. She noticed Lindsay was already up and wondered what time it was. "How is the poor dog?"

"My pa said he will be amazed if that old dog pulls through," said Robby, his hair sticking up even more than normal.

"He said we'd better be praying." Richard was now talking.

77

"You know what, Kathleen?" Now it was Robby. "Alex says he's a nice dog after all. I can't imagine who'd want to shoot a dog—even if he bit me." Robby's eyes softened as he spoke.

Kathleen sat up in bed and looked at Robby to see if he suspected that she was the guilty one, but he just kept rambling on about which neighbor might have committed the great crime.

"I'm glad it happened because Alex says if I'm really nice to Bruiser while he's sick, he'll be loyal to me and never chase or bite me ever again."

Lindsay walked into the bedroom. "That's right, Robby. Maybe he'll even want to live here with you—he could be that dog you've always dreamed of owning."

Kathleen felt her face flush at the sight of Lindsay. She wondered if she knew her secret.

"Good morning, Kathleen. I brought another heating stone for your bed." Lindsay slipped the stone under the quilts. "Mama said I should let you sleep in after your trek through the snow last night, but I see it's too late." She ruffled Robby's hair. "We tried to keep these two out of your room. They've been wanting to come up and tell you all about Bruiser ever since the crack of dawn. Breakfast will be ready in about twenty minutes."

Kathleen studied Lindsay's face before she left to see if she might suspect what had really happened. But Lindsay seemed like her normal, matter-of-fact, practical self.

Lindsay grabbed the boys and pulled them from the room. "Come on. Let's give Kathleen some privacy so she can get dressed."

Kathleen was warm under her blankets, and she wished she could stay there and not have to face the family at the breakfast table. What would they say if they knew she'd shot the dog? Even worse, what if the dog died? It would be entirely her fault.

Hoping to find comfort, Kathleen reached over to her nightstand and grabbed her Bible.

Dear Lord, I am in great need of encouragement this morning. Please lead me to just the right verse to calm my heart.

Kathleen opened her Bible and found Romans 12:12. "Be joyful in hope, patient in affliction, faithful in prayer," she read.

This certainly applied to her situation. She needed to be joyful in the hope that everything would work out, to patiently bear whatever dismal consequences her hasty actions would bring—even if it meant that Bruce thought less of her from this day forward—and then to remain faithful in prayer, asking God to be her defense. After all, she did not maliciously try to murder someone's pet. She would never do that.

Kathleen made up her mind to face the family. She nodded her head decisively and rolled out of bed. She had just completed dressing, when someone knocked on the door. It was Alex.

"Kathleen, can I talk to you for a minute?"

Kathleen's Unforgettable Winter

She felt both relieved and nervous. She knew it must have something to do with the dog and hoped that it was good news. Kathleen opened the door and tried to blink away the tears that burned the corner of her eyes without any warning.

"Yes?" Alex had the same compassionate expression that he wore the night before when he first came in with the dog.

"Kathleen, I think you've figured out by now that it wasn't a coyote that you shot," he began slowly.

"Yes, I know. I feel so terribly miserable for the poor dog. I don't think I'll ever be a farm girl." Kathleen blinked her eyes to keep the tears from falling.

"Nonsense! You are an incredible shot—a natural."

"Maybe it was a good shot, but it takes someone pretty citified to think someone's pet is a man-eating wolf just because it's running around in the woods."

Alex laughed, but Kathleen felt too miserable to see any humor in the situation.

"That's not true, Kathleen. Old Bruiser is a German shepherd. His markings look a lot like a large coyote—or even a wolf. I could have easily made the same mistake. But all that matters now is that he gets better so we can return him to his owner."

"Does that mean he's going to be okay?"

Alex shook his head. "My pa thinks it will be a close shave, but if he survives the next few days, the ol' dog might make it."

"I've been praying awfully hard. I feel terrible." Kathleen crossed her arms and hung her head.

"That's not the only reason I came up here. I told Papa the story, but he and Mama are the only ones who know what really happened—Bruce doesn't even know. Papa says he thinks you should tell your parents, but beyond that he sees no reason why everyone should know. So, unless you decide you want to tell, we can just forget about the whole thing." Alex smiled, as if he'd just presented her with a priceless gift.

No one knew? Suddenly Kathleen felt lighter. "Really! That makes me feel so much better."

Alex seemed to want to say something else to her, but she wasn't sure what. She brushed back her stubborn curl that always hung across her face. "Of course, I would never lie if someone asked me what happened. But it's nice to know that everyone doesn't have to know—at least not for a while anyway."

"We will have to explain to Mr. Johnston what happened to his dog. But, if Grandpa is right about this snowstorm," Alex looked out Lindsay's bedroom window, "we won't be going anywhere for at least a week. By that time, I'm sure Bruiser will be in great shape, and Mr. Johnston will be so relieved that he's okay, he will probably not think too hard about the fact that you mistook his dog for a wolf."

Kathleen hoped Alex was right. She dreaded the idea of having to tell Mr. Johnston that she was the one who had shot his dog. Maybe by some sort of miracle she would never have to face him. Kathleen looked at

Alex's face and knew that wasn't a very grown-up thing to be thinking.

"I'm sure I will feel better after I face Mr. Johnston with the truth. But I will not mind one bit if the storm puts that meeting off for a few days. Hopefully Bruiser will heal up so we can bring him home. I can't imagine what I would say if someone shot my dog. Lindsay told me that he is not the—well, kindest of neighbors. Do you think Mr. Johnston will believe that it was truly an accident?" Kathleen looked pleadingly up at Alex.

"Don't worry, Kathleen. It is obvious you meant no mischief. But, to be honest with you, I don't know how Mr. Johnston will respond. Let's just keep praying that Bruiser heals. He and his wife are an odd couple. They keep pretty much to themselves and prefer not to be bothered. Mrs. Johnston used to be nice enough, and she even attended church years ago with their son—that is, until he died in a farm accident. Folks say that when she lost her only child, it broke her spirit. Since then she's shut herself up in their house and no one ever sees her."

"How tragic! The poor lady . . . and now I've shot their only dog." Kathleen covered her eyes with her hands. How could they ever possibly forgive her?

"Oh, don't worry. Bruiser is Mr. Johnston's dog, and he's not dead yet. Pa cleaned the wound and dressed it best he could—we just have to pray it doesn't get infected. I'll be changing his bandages at least twice a day, so that should help." Alex leaned up against the door.

"Can I see him?"

"Papa thinks it will do Bruiser well to sleep, so he has forbidden any visitors until later this afternoon." Alex sounded more like Uncle John or her own papa at that moment, but Kathleen was grateful. She knew he was just being a protective older cousin.

"Can I at least help you change his bandages?" Kathleen pleaded.

"I'll let you help me later this evening. But he's fine for now, and breakfast is sure smelling good." Alex patted Kathleen on the shoulder. "Why don't you try not to fret and come down and get a bite to eat?"

"Thank you so much, Alex." Kathleen followed him down to join the family at the table, but she felt so sick to her stomach that the thought of breakfast did not sit too well. All she really wanted to do was check on the dog and try to nurse him back to health.

They had barely started breakfast when Uncle John announced that the night's snowstorm had let up quite a bit, but he feared the worse was yet to come.

"Grandpa says his bad knee is worse than ever." Uncle John piled a stack of hotcakes on his plate. "He thinks we're in for a bad snowstorm, maybe even a blizzard. I'll need all hands on deck. We need to get ready for the long haul. I think everyone needs to move from Grandpa and Grandma's house into ours—that way we'll burn half the wood. The extra bodies inside will help keep us warmer too. You never know how long a

storm like this will last — we must be prepared for the worst." Uncle John took a bite of sausage. His bushy eyebrows furrowed deep in thought.

Kathleen thought it was a little odd to trust her grandpa's knee as an accurate weather report, but she could sense Uncle John's apprehension about the storm that was headed their way.

Uncle John pointed at Alex and Bruce with his fork. "Boys, as soon as Grandpa finishes reading the Bible after breakfast is over, I want you to go fetch wood from the pile out back and stack it in the kitchen and on the back porch. I need the rest of you to help insulate the house with loads of hay."

"Hay?" Bruce looked a bit surprised as he buttered his toast.

Grandma Maggie looked up from stoking the stove, old Mary Washington, with a look of concern written across her brow.

"Yes, I know," said Uncle John. "One spark and the whole house could go up in flames. We will have to keep it away from the stove and hearth to make sure it doesn't catch fire." Uncle John passed the bowl of soft boiled eggs to Aunt Elizabeth. "Your grandpa, Uncle James, and I have been talking about how thin our wood floors are. And insulating them with hay is about the only thing we've come up with to keep the heat from escaping."

"What will we do with the hay once we have it inside?" Lindsay asked as she spread a generous amount of peach jam on her hotcakes.

"We'll pull all the rugs up and lay the hay down underneath," Grandpa said.

"And then what?" Kathleen looked at her papa.

"Then we'll have a trampling party and stomp it all down till it's packed nice and thick." Papa winked at Kathleen. "When we put the rugs back down, we figure we'll have a padded, warm floor to walk on." Papa held out his coffee cup and Mama refilled it.

Lindsay still looked confused.

Aunt Elizabeth tried to explain, "We will sew burlap bags together to cover the floors in the rooms that don't have rugs—which is virtually all of them, except the front parlor. But before we do that, we will have to get the hay inside, before the snow starts again. Otherwise, we'll have wet hay on our floor that could very well freeze before it dries out." Aunt Elizabeth shivered and wrapped her arms around herself more tightly.

Even though it didn't help her stay any warmer, Kathleen was glad that she was not the only one who considered this weather unusually cold.

The Race Against the Blizzard

*Perseverance must finish its work so that you may be
mature and complete, not lacking anything.*

JAMES 1:4

After a hurried breakfast, everyone went in his or her own direction, each with the common goal of preparing for the blizzard as quickly as possible. There was a general feeling of excitement in the air mixed with anxiety. Kathleen had overheard her aunt say that she was thankful that they had plenty of food due to the large deer Bruce had just shot, but she feared for the neighbors who might not have been as blessed.

The chilling winds began picking up and snow clouds gathered in the distance. Kathleen and Lindsay wrapped up tightly and rushed out to the barn to help, the new snow crunching under their feet. Uncle John and Papa had already hitched the large draft horses, Dan and Daisy, to the wagon and were inside the barn tossing huge pitchforksful of hay into it from the loft.

"Girls, jump into the wagon and stomp down the hay while we fill it," Uncle John shouted down to them on the ground. Kathleen was glad to have a job that would keep her moving. It was so cold it hurt to breathe. The girls jumped and bounced around, dodging the large clumps of straw that her papa and uncle tossed from the loft, packing down the hay until the wagon was full.

Papa laughed at their appearance. Bits of dried grass and straw covered them from head to foot. "You two look like you've been tarred and feathered. What was the crime?"

Kathleen immediately thought about the poor dog that was lying in the pantry, and the sick feeling in her stomach came back. The neighbor who owned him may want to tar and feather her when he found out what she had done.

Dear Lord, please, please, heal Ol' Bruiser.

Kathleen looked up at her papa. The morning had been so busy that she had not had time to tell him about her deed yet. She wished she could tell him now. He always had a way of making things look brighter. Even though Kathleen had repeated Romans 12:12 over and over again all morning and resolved to be joyful in hope, she still felt miserable inside.

"Joyful in hope, patient in affliction, faithful in prayer . . ." she repeated to herself as she worked.

87

Kathleen forced herself to smile and slid off the hay wagon to the barn floor.

Lindsay gathered the hay that had slid down with them. "Kathleen, help me. We can put this extra straw in Nelly's stall. I want to make sure that she and the filly stay warm."

Kathleen shook her head doubtfully as she spread the soft yellow material in the stall. It was so cold she wondered if it would even help. The filly stood on its wobbly little legs and looked curiously at Kathleen with big, docile brown eyes. Then, as if to let Kathleen know that she was not perceived as a threat, Doll nickered, sending white steam out of her velvety nose.

"She likes you all right! Not many foals take to humans so quickly." Lindsay laughed with delight at the warm reception Kathleen received.

"Do you think she'll survive the storm?" Kathleen asked. She was already getting quite attached to Doll and did not like the thought of her suffering.

"Papa says she'll be fine. Even so, I can't help but worry a bit. If it gets as bad as Grandpa says . . ."

"Girls, I'll meet you at the house," Uncle John called from the hay wagon. "We need to get this hay inside. The wind is picking up, and I am afraid that time is running out. The blizzard will be here before we know it!" He cracked his whip at the horses. Papa swung the barn doors open. The strong wind caught the huge doors and flung them hard against the barn walls. The loud bang startled the animals inside and there was

much mooing, nickering, and cackling. Kathleen wrapped her wool scarf around her face. The gust of cold air that howled through the barn was enough to make even the bravest heart tremble in its icy grip.

The next few hours everyone in the family raced to fortify the house and barn before the storm hit.

Uncle John seemed to have a list ingrained in his mind. There were the animals to feed and water, firewood to stack, hay to spread over the floor of the house, meat to gather from the smokehouse, and buckets of drinking water to carry in from the pump outside. He even asked Kathleen and Lindsay to attach a long rope from the back porch leading to the barn door, just in case the blizzard became blinding. That way he still would have a way to find the animals; after all, the cows would need to be milked every day or they'd stop producing milk. And without milk, there would be no cream or butter or cottage cheese.

Aunt Elizabeth, Grandma Maggie, and Mama had their own lists of things for Lindsay and Kathleen to do. There were canned goods, potatoes, onions, and beets to collect from the root cellar, and extra candles, kerosene lamps and oil, and quilts to gather from Grandma Maggie's house.

Kathleen thought the storm would not be so frightening if they had electricity and a furnace to heat the house, like they had in Fort Wayne—but since this was where God had them, she was glad that Uncle John was experienced in storm preparation. She was beginning to realize

if they did not prepare properly they could freeze in their own home.

Even Richard and Robby had jobs. They gathered buckets of snow and put them in wash tubs to melt by the hearth. In case of fire, Uncle John said. The water would be good to have on hand just in case a spark or two were to leap from the stove and catch the floor on fire. The little boys also carried in firewood and piled it next to the stove, old Mary Washington, and the fireplace.

Alex and Bruce were primarily responsible for all the barn chores and seemed to know exactly what needed to be done without any prompting.

Lindsay and Kathleen spread a thick layer of hay across the floors. Next, they helped stretch the rugs and burlap over the top of it until all the floors were covered. Papa and Uncle John held the carpet in place while the children jumped and stomped the mounds of hay, filling the house with the sweet smell of hay.

Grandpa McKenzie joined them and pretended to do a Scottish fling, making everyone laugh.

"What is so funny?" Grandpa asked. "If it wasn't for my wee jig, your Grandma Maggie and I may not have ever been married." He winked at Grandma, who was sitting across the room on the sofa with Aunt Elizabeth and Mama. They were in front of the fireplace frantically sewing burlap sacks together.

Grandma Maggie put her work down in her lap, brushed back a loose strand of white hair that had

90

escaped from her loosely worn bun, and said with a determined smile, "Now Jim, just because all the other lassies on the boat to America were impressed, doesn't mean I even noticed your dancing skills. I've told you before, it wasn't until you risked your life to save an older woman who was almost washed overboard during that terrible storm, that I truly realized you were a man of courage and character—a true gentleman."

"Come now, Maggie! After all these years you still won't admit I swept you off your feet with the first of the many Scottish reels that helped to pass the long, weary hours of the journey?" Grandpa repeated his jig and bowed to his "bonnie lass."

Kathleen observed her grandpa's strong-featured face framed by his thick gray hair and bushy sideburns and thought how handsome he must have been in his younger days.

"You know very well, Jim, that I never danced with you until after you proved yourself a true man by laying your life down for that old granny. And yes, I do admit that you did sweep me off my feet on that first reel. In fact, I'm not so sure I ever landed back on the ground again." Grandma Maggie smiled wistfully and then shook her head with a girlish laugh.

"Tell us more, Grandpa!" begged Kathleen as she jumped up and down. "I knew that you and Grandma Maggie met on a boat when you were emigrating from Scotland to America, but I've never heard any of these details."

91

Kathleen's Unforgettable Winter

"Not now, my little lassie. Tonight, after our work is done. I can hear the wind picking up. Soon the blizzard will be so severe that we will have no choice but to sit around telling stories." Grandpa stomped down the hay and before long everyone was hard at work again.

Kathleen looked around the room and noticed how dark it was, even though it was only a little past three o'clock.

Shortly afterward Uncle John announced that all that could be done was done. "We may as well get comfortable. The storm is here and it's not going to get any warmer. Elizabeth, before you ladies start supper, make sure to ration out the food supply to last at least a week. You never know how long this storm will take to run its course."

The snow was coming down with such fury that it looked dim outside, leaving the glowing hearth fire the only thing that lit the family room. The wind was so mighty that it roared against the house. Kathleen was tired from all the work, but Robby and Richard still bounced up and down on the floor, insisting that there was a lumpy spot beneath. But everyone knew that it was mostly an excuse to run and jump in the house, something that was normally forbidden.

Kathleen sighed. It was the first time all day that she had time to go check on the dog that was lying injured in the kitchen pantry. Uncle John and Alex had checked on him throughout the day and told her they thought he was holding up, but Kathleen wanted to see

him for herself. She wondered how bad he looked. Would he live? How would she ever face his owner? Kathleen hoped that Uncle John would let her visit Bruiser soon.

Finally, Alex pulled Kathleen aside and told her it was time for her to go visit Bruiser herself. She quietly slipped out of the living room, then made her way through the kitchen and into the pantry beyond. It was cold and dark, but Kathleen could see a dark lump in the corner. It was bigger than she thought, but it must be the dog. She moved a bit closer. Much to her surprise, the lump stood up to a man's full height.

"Papa, is that you?" Kathleen blinked, trying to help her eyes adjust to the darkness. She noticed that he held a lantern in his hand, but it was not lit. "Why don't you light your lantern?"

"I just blew it out, hoping Bruiser would rest. You see, I was examining Bruiser's battle wounds and noticed that, well—Kathleen, about that coyote you shot . . ."

Kathleen hung her head. She knew her papa had figured things out and wished that she had already told him the truth.

Life's Lessons

Let us fix our eyes on Jesus, the author and perfecter of our faith,
who for the joy set before him endured the cross, scorning its shame,
and sat down at the right hand of the throne of God.

Kathleen felt ashamed over the mishap with the dog. She hoped her papa would understand that it was an accident. Papa walked over to her and lifted her chin gently with his strong hand. "It is not like my lass to keep a secret."

"I wanted to talk to you, Papa, but things have been so crazy—we've not had a single moment by ourselves until now. I—I shot the dog." The pantry was too dark to see clearly, but Kathleen knew her papa was looking lovingly into her eyes. "I was just so sure that he was one of those man-eating wolves you told me about. Alex said it was just a coyote. But when he took a closer look, he found things were a little different." Kathleen hung her head again. No matter how innocent of a mistake, she still felt awful about the whole thing.

"Kathleen, don't be ashamed. I did not ask you about it to scold you. I just wanted you to be open. I want you to know that your mama and I will always be here to support and encourage you in life—no matter what sort of catastrophe you might find yourself in. I know the Lord will give you the courage to tell your cousins what happened."

Kathleen hugged her papa. "Thanks, Papa." His love filled her heart and eased the guilt she had been feeling. She wished then she had come to him sooner. If only they lived in the same house. If only she could walk down the hallway to his bedroom, like she used to do in Fort Wayne. He released her and ran his finger down her nose in his loving way.

"How is Bruiser? I've been so worried," Kathleen asked, kneeling down by the dog. She held her hand out so he could sniff it. Bruiser lifted his head and licked Kathleen's hand. She gently stroked his coat.

"He's stable right now. We just need to watch for any infection. That could make his situation pretty grim."

"Papa, I wanted so much to prove myself to my cousins—especially Bruce. He thought I was a prissy city girl. I might have grown up in the city, but that doesn't mean I'm afraid to get my hands dirty." Kathleen clenched her jaw and straightened her shoulders. She was determined to be brave and keep her emotions in check. She ran her fingers up and down the green fringe of her dress pocket.

Papa sat down on the floor next to Kathleen and Bruiser. "I know a lot has changed in your life in such a short time. You have left everything familiar behind, and farm life must feel like living in a different country. And on top of that, you are not even sleeping in the same house as Mama and me. I know all of this has been a hard adjustment, but I want you to know that I am so proud of you for being so brave."

"I wish Bruce thought so—he was impressed with my shooting, but if he finds out that I was the one who shot the dog, he will probably never let me live it down."

"Hmmm. I was about to say that I was proud of you in everything, but one little area." Papa rubbed his chin thoughtfully.

"What, Papa? What else have I done?" Kathleen could not stand the thought of making her papa displeased with her in any way.

"I keep hearing you express how important it is for you to prove yourself and how you want others to think well of you. That is natural and quite understandable— especially when you are in a new environment and want to fit in. But, do you think that perhaps you might have some pride in your heart?"

"Pride?"

"Yes, if you did not have any pride you would not be worried about what Bruce thought of you."

"I—I guess that's really what it is, isn't it? It's just that I don't want anyone to think badly of me." Kathleen's voice drifted off. She rubbed Bruiser behind his ears.

"I understand. It's a normal human desire, but no matter how hard you try in life, you will never be able to please everyone.

"The important thing is that you ask yourself if you are pleasing God, not man. If you know that your actions are pure before God, then you shouldn't care what other people think. Remember the McKenzie family motto: 'we shine, not burn'? We are to shine for Christ—nothing else really matters."

"You are right that I am concerned about what other people think." Kathleen sighed. "I will try to focus more on what God thinks of me, rather than Bruce or anyone else." Kathleen's eyes burned and she fought back the tears. "I'm sorry for being so prideful." She knew her papa was right, but for some reason she still cared a lot about what her cousins thought of her and wanted to feel accepted more than anything.

"Papa, I will try to not worry about fitting in."

"That's my bonnie lass. Maybe when school starts—"

"Oh, Papa, that's something else that is burdening my heart," Kathleen said. "I don't want to get behind in my education like Lindsay and . . . well . . . I *am* still studying for the National Spelling Bee. Is it—too much for me to dream that it might work out?" The tears now streamed down her face.

Papa held Kathleen for some time before he answered. "Do you remember our devotional last summer on running the race of life?"

Kathleen nodded silently against Papa's strong chest.

"We spoke of the challenge of the sudden changes and trials that often come in life—that sometimes you may be running strong and carefree on the mountain of blessing and then—"

"Then all of a sudden your whole world might change and you may find yourself in the dark valley of sorrow . . . and it's not the stumbling that disqualifies you, it's the failure to get up and keep on running. Yes, I remember—all too well." Kathleen put her cheek upon his rough wool shirt.

Papa stroked her hair. "You took a tumble during the race, didn't you?" he said. "I will never forget how proud I was of my daughter that day. You persevered to the end despite the obstacles that were hindering you from your course. However, there is yet another lesson that can be drawn from Hebrews 12:1–2. In fact it is the very next verse, and it goes hand in hand with running the race of life. After the words 'let us run with perseverance the race marked out for us,' it goes on to say, 'fix our eyes on Jesus, the author and perfecter of our faith, who for the joy set before him endured the cross.'"

"What does that have to do with the spelling bee?" Kathleen asked.

"It applies in every way, each day of your life. You see, if you view Jesus Christ as the 'Author and Finisher of your faith,' you view Him as the One who is in control of your life and the One who has written the next chapter. When you read a mystery or adventure novel, you are often left in suspense to know what will happen next, or why such a heart-wrenching thing could happen to the main character. Many times you are left in a great quandary until the end of the book. Then everything ties together and makes perfect sense."

Bruiser whined from his bed in the pantry. Papa went over and gently ran his fingers down the dog's side. "That is just like our lives. God is the ultimate author and He has already intricately and masterfully written the story of your life. Though you might not understand why He allows something in this chapter, you must trust that the twists and turns that He places in your path are weaving together the ultimate plot for your life into His perfect will. This is often hard for us to do on our own; that's why God calls us to keep our eyes fixed on Him. As it says in Hebrews 12:1, we must choose to throw off doubt, worry, fear, bitterness, and anything else that might hinder us from running the race with perseverance, and focus on trusting God's faithfulness. It says we are surrounded by a great cloud, or a vast number, of witnesses—men and women who have gone before us and already know the end of their script. They have run their races, endured to the end, and know that God was faithful on their behalf." Papa brushed back the curl that Kathleen's stubborn cowlick always placed across her forehead and lifted her chin to look her straight in her eyes.

"I cannot promise you that we will be able to go to Washington, D.C., in the spring—it will all depend on my finding a job. But I can promise you that your Heavenly Papa knows what the next chapter holds, and even if that means we do not have the money to travel, you can trust His will and His timing. Who knows, maybe you will be the First Lady someday and live in the White House. He has obviously planted a desire in your heart to see our nation's capital—you never can tell what His ultimate will is for your life. As Christians, our responsibility is merely to trust and obey."

That night, before Kathleen blew out her lamp, she picked her Bible off the nightstand and pulled out the newspaper clipping with her picture and placed it over her heart. *Dear Lord, I really do want to go to the National Spelling Bee, but I know that times are hard and that it might be too expensive to travel all the way to Washington, D.C. You know my desire to go, Lord Jesus, but please help me to trust You, no matter what happens. But most of all, Lord, please help Papa find a job so we can return home.*

Kathleen pressed her face against the glass windowpane and tried to catch a glimmer of light outside. According to Papa's silver pocket watch, it was already evening, but to Kathleen or anyone else in the house,

they could not tell the difference — it could have been anytime, day or night.

The blizzard had not let up for two days. At first, Kathleen had doubted her grandpa's and uncle's ability to predict the weather so accurately, but now she was glad they had made such an effort to fortify the wood supply and line the floors with hay.

"Can't see much, can you?" Alex whispered in Kathleen's ear.

Startled, she jumped. She had not heard him coming up behind her. "No — I can't see much at all. In fact, I can't see anything."

"That's because between the drifts and the snow falling off the roof, the window is completely covered."

"Are you serious? I've never seen such a storm. Do you think it will *ever* stop?" Kathleen rubbed the glass with the palm of her hand.

"The snow reached the top of the windows hours ago. But I wouldn't worry about it — that is, I wouldn't be worried unless it gets higher than the upstairs windows. Then we'd really be snowed in."

Kathleen shuddered. She looked around the cozy room, lit by oil lamps, and tried to comfort herself in the warmth of the fire and of her family who surrounded her. No one else seemed worried. Papa and Mama sat at the dining room table. Papa was reading a week-old newspaper and Mama was sipping a cup of coffee and scanning the articles of interest that Papa passed on to her.

Kathleen's Unforgettable Winter

At the other end of the table, Uncle John and Aunt Elizabeth played a game of chess. Robby, Richard, and Lindsay were engrossed in a game of jacks on the floor.

Kathleen looked fondly at Grandma Maggie, who was sitting in a rocking chair near the hearth. She was knitting a wool sweater as she rocked. Kathleen wondered if she ever stopped working—even when Grandma Maggie was sitting, her fingers were busy with one task or another. Her fingers flew, causing the "click, click" of her knitting needles and "creak, crock" of the rocking chair to blend in a soothing harmony.

Papa glanced up at her and something in his eyes reminded her that she still had to tell her cousins that she was the one who had shot Bruiser. She swallowed hard as a wave of fear tightened her throat.

She had missed an opportunity to tell Bruce when she helped Alex and him clean and change the dressing on Old Bruiser's wound. Bruiser seemed to be improving, but they were still holding their breath, praying that an infection would not set in.

Maybe when she knew he was going to be okay, she would tell them then. Now did not seem to be the best time, with everyone looking so peaceful. Lindsay interrupted Kathleen's thoughts.

"Grandpa, remember the story you promised to tell us?" asked Lindsay.

"Oh yes, Grandpa, please tell us," Kathleen said as she looked up at Grandpa, who sat near Kathleen. He stopped whittling the small wooden boat he had been

working on and gazed at the fire with a faraway look in his eye.

Kathleen longed to hear how Grandma Maggie and he fell in love and why they left Scotland. She could not imagine what would make two people want to leave their homeland, travel across the sea, and start a new life in another country. She was having a hard enough time adjusting to her move from Indiana to Ohio.

"Come, dear," said Grandma as she motioned to Kathleen. "Sit here between us. It's time you heard what really happened."

Grandma Maggie's Love Story

*As the heavens are higher than the earth, so are my ways higher
than your ways and my thoughts than your thoughts.*

ISAIAH 55:9

Kathleen sat on the floor between
Grandma Maggie's rocker and Grandpa's
chair, with Lindsay next to her. She could
feel the lumpy hay beneath her and the
smell of it filled the house with an aroma
like the barn, but she didn't mind. They were comfortable. The glow of the hearth warmed her face.

"That fire sure does make your red hair shine," said
Grandma, reaching out to touch it.

Kathleen gazed into the fire for some time, not really
sure how to ask all the questions that loomed in her mind.

Grandma Maggie laid her knitting in her lap. "You
know, I too had to leave everything familiar behind and
adjust to a completely different life when I was your age."

Grandma Maggie looked at Kathleen with such a
kind and understanding expression that Kathleen knew

she could tell Grandma Maggie anything she was struggling with and she would understand. A lump formed in her throat, but Kathleen swallowed hard. In her determination not to cry, she blurted out, "You were my age when you moved to America? But I thought you said you and Grandpa . . .? Weren't you too young to get married?" She looked at Grandpa, who had picked up his knife and was whittling away on the toy boat.

"No, no, dearie. I was a young lass of eighteen when I met your Grandpa." Grandma picked up her needles and skillfully worked as she talked. "That was my second big move. The first one was when I was a wee lass about your age. You see, I'm a Scotch-Irish girl, and my father's family lived on a farm in Northern Ireland for generations. My mother was from Scotland, and when she married my father, they settled on his family's farm. My parents were the only folks in my family to stick with farming and survive the great hardships of the Irish potato famine. I'm told that most of the families left Ireland to start a new life in America, but I was not even a twinkle in my daddy's eye back then, so I don't know for sure. I was not born until 1858, a good eight years after the worst of it."

The wind howled outside, making the whole house creak and shudder. Kathleen inched closer to the hearth fire.

Grandma continued, "My own folks, though, told me they were determined to persevere and stay with the land that our family had farmed for years. Somehow they managed, but it cost them everything. Mother always told me that the four years of famine aged Father at least twenty years. In the midst of it all, my father lost most of his savings and never again recovered the money.

"As a wee lassie, I worked the land alongside my parents and two younger brothers, William and Douggie, from dawn to dusk. No matter how hard we worked, it was never enough. Many a night, I went to bed hungry—there wasn't enough food to go around. Imagine this, dearie." Grandma Maggie stopped knitting, and her face turned to stone at the memory. "My brothers would squabble over whose turn it was to eat the top of my father's boiled egg. And I remember being merry just getting the crust of the bread. We considered it to be the best piece—not like so many of you lads 'n' lassies today that turn your noses up at it." Grandma Maggie sighed and her face softened.

Bruce added a few more logs to the fire and stood there stoking it until it cracked and snapped. He pretended not to be listening, but Kathleen could tell he wanted to hear the story too.

"Despite the hardships, for the most part, I remember being happy." She resumed knitting and rocking. "No amount of wealth or riches can buy a happy childhood. I was rich because my family was together, and I knew they loved me dearly."

Kathleen turned to see Richard and Robbie disappearing up the stairs. She was surprised they didn't want to stay and hear the story.

Grandpa followed her gaze and shook his head and started to get up. "I smell trouble in the air."

"Maybe I ought to go see what they're up to," said Grandma, laying aside her knitting.

"Please don't stop," begged Kathleen. "I'm sure they're just after a new game."

Grandma didn't seem convinced, but she settled back in her chair. "Let's see, where was I? Oh, yes. I was 'rich' until one day, when I was just a bit younger than you, Kathleen, an epidemic swept through the town near us. One of Mother's friends took sick. My dear mither always thought of others before being concerned for herself. Without a second thought, she was at Mrs. Ferguson's sickbed, nursing her back to health." Grandma Maggie stopped her knitting a moment and gazed long and hard into the fire.

Kathleen could tell she was trying to hold back tears. Kathleen looked down at the floor and started picking at pieces of straw that had worked their way through the seams in the burlap. Seeing her Grandma Maggie's sadness made Kathleen want to cry. She wished she knew how to comfort her.

Grandma Maggie wiped away a tear, took a deep breath, and began rocking again. "Even though her friend pulled through, Mother came down with the illness shortly after leaving Mrs. Ferguson's sickbed. The week that followed is still a blur in my mind, but I know that both Mither and Daddy died and were buried before I even accepted the fact that they were

sick. As I said before, my father was out of money, and there was no way that my younger brothers and I could manage the farm by ourselves, so it was sold." Grandma sighed deeply. "My brothers and I were shipped off to Scotland to our uncle's home, my mother's oldest brother. We had never met him, and I'm afraid he never forgave my mother for marrying an Irishman. It was soon obvious he wished he had never met us. William and Douggie were there only a week when he announced that he would be spending the money from the sale of the farm to ship my two brothers to another relative's farm in America. He said we had an uncle there who would put my wee brothers to work, and they would have to earn their own room and board.

" 'It might even make men out of you two bairns,' he had said gruffly.

"Much to my dismay, he informed me there would be no use for me on the farm. Instead, he placed me in a Scottish boarding school in Glasgow. I pleaded and begged him not to separate us, but it was no use. He packed my precious few belongings and sent me off to Stonewyke Boarding School, assuring me that my schoolin' would be covered with the money from the farm. He must have kept a good portion for himself because the school informed me just before my graduation that they hadn't received payment from him in over a year. They told me that I'd have to work an extra two years to pay back the debt.

"By then I had not seen my brothers in over three years, and all I wanted to do was earn enough money to book my passage to America. I was determined to find my wee brothers. You can only imagine the anguish in my heart when I learned I would have to wait at least another two years."

Grandma Maggie's story was suddenly interrupted by a thundering noise that came from the stairwell. Kathleen jumped to her feet. Her first thought was that the roof had caved in from the weight of the snow; then she realized that there was muffled laughter and squeals of glee in the midst of the thundering. A large cloth bag appeared at the bottom of the stairs. Aunt Elizabeth stood over it with her hands on her hips as two little boys peered out of a sleeping bag lying at her feet.

"I do declare," said Aunt Elizabeth, "I thought there was a herd of cattle coming down those steps. Heaven only knows what you boys will come up with next. The sooner this storm ends and the two of you get outdoors the better."

"I'm sorry, Aunt Elizabeth," Richard said as he and Robby crawled out of the sleeping bag they'd used as a sled. "Our staircase at our home back in Fort Wayne isn't nearly as fun. I've been wanting to try it out here ever since we arrived. It works pretty good—you just have to make sure you keep your body straight as an arrow." Richard rubbed a spot on the seat of his pants where it obviously hurt.

"Looks like he didn't straighten his body enough," said Lindsay.

Kathleen looked back at Grandma Maggie, let out a sigh of relief, and sank back down to her spot on the floor. She was glad that it was just the boys and not the whole roof caving in. Kathleen began to imagine how hard it would be to be separated from Richard. He might be an energetic, sometimes mischievous little boy, but Kathleen loved him dearly. She looked back at Grandma Maggie.

"Did you ever find your brothers?" Kathleen asked.

Once again, her grandma got a distant look in her eyes as though she were peering back in time. "My mother was a God-fearing woman and taught me to pray as a child, but when she and Father died and my brothers and I were separated, I determined that God must not have been hearing my prayers. If He did, I figured that He definitely did not care for me. After all, if God cared, He would not allow such hardships in my life—or at least that's what I thought. So I decided that if God wasn't helping me, I would have to survive on my own and make my own way in the world. I became very bitter toward my uncle and trusted no one—not even the headmistress at the boarding school.

"There was only one person who befriended me during those years that I truly felt I could trust. It was old Annie, the school's cook. She was a kind, older lady whose loving heart was as big as her plump frame. Annie was a Christian woman, and though I grew to love her,

I refused to hear anything about the Heavenly Father's love. When I finally worked off my debt, she insisted I go board with her cousin while I earned my wages for the boat fare. I thanked Annie for her kindness, took the cousin's address, and left, determined to make it on my own. The next months were the hardest and loneliest of my life. I scoured the countryside for work. There I was, seventeen years old, homeless, virtually penniless, and without any kin I could call my own.

"One winter evening, while traveling to the town of Stirling, I was caught in a snowstorm. It was a brutal storm, and I thought I was near the end, but thankfully, I happened upon a wee roadside town and sought shelter before it was too late. I did not have the strength to go on and knew I would catch a death of cold if I didn't find help."

Kathleen shivered and scooted closer to the fire. Outside, the howling blizzard winds were so fierce that sometimes the whole house frame shook and added to the story, making Kathleen feel that she were right there in Scotland with her Grandma Maggie so many years before.

"Wet, cold, and hungry, I stumbled to a sheltered spot in a corner between two buildings on the deserted high street of the town. There, I slumped down into a ball on the ground. Plunging my hands deep within the pockets of my thin jacket, I felt a piece of paper. It was the paper that Annie the cook had given me with the name and address of her friend.

" 'Dear God,' I cried feebly. 'If You are truly real . . . and if . . . if You care about me, please save me. I've tried hard to make it on my own and I can't take it anymore. Please help me. Help my wee brothers . . .'

"The next thing I remember is waking up in a cozy warm, soft bed with clean white sheets. There was a kind-faced, old wifey hovering over me, gently caring for me. At first I wondered if I had died and gone to Heaven. Perhaps this kind wifey was an angel. Gradually I came to, and the lady introduced herself to me as Mrs. Randall. A passerby had spotted me curled up in the corner and found the address crumpled up in my hand. In God's great providence, the town that I had stumbled into happened to be the very town that Mrs. Randall lived in, so the man immediately brought me to Mrs. Randall's lodging.

"Evidently I had been delirious for several days, but Mrs. Randall nursed me back to health. I was weak and suffered from a severe chest cold for several weeks after that. Many times I would awake to the sweet sound of Mrs. Randall's voice as she sang a hymn or read Scriptures to me. I found a new hunger to know Christ. It grew within me each day, and gradually I began to pray to God as naturally as I spoke with Mrs. Randall.

"I lived with her for nearly a year while working as a tutor for a rich English family with a large country estate near the town. During that time, Mrs. Randall became almost like a mother to me and spent many hours mentoring me in my newfound faith in God. But there was one thing that was holding me back—bitterness toward my uncle. No matter how hard I tried, I could not forgive him. Mrs. Randall assured me that God works everything out for the best—even the difficulties in life—but I could not see how that was possible. I could not imagine how God could take the heartless act of my uncle and turn it into good in my life. But God did have a plan in it all—I just needed to trust Him and wait to see His will unfold. So I worked, saved my money, and finally set out on my journey.

"I left Scotland with just enough money in my pocket to make it to Ohio, where I last heard that my brothers lived.

"So it was that I boarded the ship, *The Queen Mary*, and headed across the great Atlantic. It was not until I left the old country behind that I began to see God's hand in my life and His purpose in allowing me to be separated from my brothers for so many years. You see, God had a whole new life waiting for me across the sea. If it wasn't for that journey, I might never have found a place I call home. I would have missed out on the biggest blessing of my life." Grandma Maggie stopped knitting and smiled at Grandpa.

Grandpa had been so focused on whittling, that Kathleen figured he had not heard a word of the story. But at the mention of when he and Grandma first met, his weathered, old face lit up, and his blue eyes twinkled. "That's when my little jig won her heart," Grandpa said.

Kathleen's Unforgettable Winter

Kathleen sat up on her knees and clasped her hands together. "Was it love at first sight, Grandpa? And what's the story of you saving that elderly lady from falling overboard?" she asked eagerly.

"Of course it was love at first sight. Your Grandma Maggie was by far the loveliest, most pure-hearted bonnie lass I had ever seen—she still is, I might add. Now, as for saving the older lady, I merely did what any man would do in the same situation. Somehow, God used it to turn your Grandma Maggie's heart toward mine. We were married just two weeks after setting foot on American soil, a wonder I never did understand." Grandpa shook his head in awe as if he still could not believe that she actually chose to marry him.

"So what about your brothers?" Kathleen asked.

"A warm smile filled Grandma's face. "Eventually I was able to find the family farm and what a joyous reunion I had with my youngest brother, William. I was saddened to find out that my other brother, Douggie, had died two years before of pneumonia. However, I was grateful to find that, unlike our uncle in Scotland, my Uncle George in America was a good Christian man. He raised my brothers as his own children. Uncle George hired your grandpa to work on his farm until we were able to purchase land of our own. And that is the story of how we got here. It took perseverance and learning the importance of giving thanks in every situation—no matter how hard—and having an abiding trust in our Savior. But God did eventually bring us out of the desert to the

Land of Promise." Grandma Maggie sat back, obviously finished with her story, and soon the "click, click" of her knitting needles and the "creak, crock" of the rocking chair filled the room once again. Grandpa stood and stoked the fire.

Kathleen stared into the sparking hearth. Grandma Maggie's story had intrigued her at first, but now she was thinking much deeper. All of a sudden, her recent hardships and trials seemed small in comparison.

If God could use Grandma Maggie's childhood tragedy for the best, surely He had a plan for her life as well, like Papa had said. There must be some good that could come out of shooting the neighbor's dog.

Kathleen tried to find a reason to be grateful, and before long she remembered that Uncle John had said that Old Bruiser was a ferocious watchdog that had threatened to spook their horses every time their wagon drove by. But now that they were nursing the dog back to health, he was becoming friends with the whole family. If God could work her shooting Old Bruiser out for good, then He *must* have a plan for Papa losing his job too. As hard as it was to believe right now, there must be a good reason for her to leave her friends and home in Fort Wayne to live on the farm and to possibly even miss the National Spelling Bee. All she needed to do was trust God and wait.

10

Old Bruiser

The LORD is my light and my salvation — whom shall I fear?
The LORD is the stronghold of my life — of whom shall I be afraid?
PSALM 27:1

"Kathleen, Lindsay," Bruce asked on the third day of the storm, "do you two feel up to braving the blizzard and joining Alex and me this afternoon with the barn chores?" Bruce pulled a warm sweater over his head. "That little filly's growing like a weed. Each time Alex and I go to feed and water the livestock and milk the cows, Doll looks like she's grown a little more."

Kathleen jumped up from the kitchen table where she and Lindsay were studying Kathleen's American history book. Lindsay's mind had not been on her studies and Kathleen had been having a hard time getting her to concentrate. At Bruce's suggestion her face brightened, as if he'd just announced it was Christmas.

"I'll go get some extra sweaters and stockings so we can layer up," Lindsay called over her shoulder as she darted up the stairs to her room.

Kathleen laughed as she watched her go. She realized how much Lindsay must have been missing Doll and maybe even worrying about her over the past few days. She'd been so wrapped up in her own worries, she hadn't given a thought to Lindsay's.

"I'd love to—let me run and ask my papa if he minds." She closed her history book.

Kathleen found Papa reading his Bible on the living room sofa. Old Bruiser rested at his feet on the sweet-smelling, hay-stuffed floor. He picked up his head and feebly wagged his tail when Kathleen entered. She slowly knelt down beside him and rubbed behind his ears.

"You look like you're gaining more and more strength every time I see you." Kathleen looked up at her papa. "And it looks like you have a new friend."

"Yes, ever since I moved him in here from the pantry this morning, he seems happiest when I'm near him." Papa closed his Bible and patted the dog on the head. "He actually whined earlier today when I went out to the barn to help your Uncle John water the livestock."

"I'm glad he's doing better—you do think he will live, don't you, Papa?" Kathleen tenderly massaged Bruiser's head and neck.

"I have not seen any signs of infection—so I'd say he has a good chance. But only time will tell. That reminds me, have you told your cousins yet, about the shooting?"

Kathleen hung her head. "No, Papa. I haven't. I've been waiting for just the right moment."

He cupped his hand under her chin and lifted her head. "The longer you put it off, the harder it will be. The sooner you tell them the better. You'll feel so much better when you do."

"You're right, Papa. I'll do it soon."

Mama strode into the room, nervously twisting one of the strings from her apron. "Kathleen, I hear you and Lindsay are going to the barn with Bruce and Alex." She looked questioningly at Papa. "James, are you sure it's safe? I heard Bruce say that the snow is gusting so much that you can't see two feet in front of you."

"That's what I was coming in here to ask you about, Papa. Bruce invited us to go to the barn so we could see Doll and help with the afternoon chores." Kathleen stood up, smoothing the wrinkles from the waistline of her dress. "May I go—I would so love to." Kathleen looked at her mama, who was still fingering her apron in apprehension. "I will be very careful not to let go of the rope that leads to the barn."

"Your mama is right; it is dangerous. Between the deep snow drifts and the strong wind gusts, a girl your size could disappear in a heartbeat." Papa stood up and took Kathleen's hand. "Tell you what—I'll go with you. I feel like stretching my legs—besides, the boys need help chopping the ice out of the water troughs so the animals can drink."

"Thanks, Papa!" Kathleen squeezed his hand.

Lindsay appeared then, carrying a bundle of clothes. "Here, Kathleen, I've brought lots of warm things for us to wear."

The trip to the barn was far more tiring than Kathleen had imagined. She was grateful to have her papa by her side as they fought their way through the deep drifts. In places it was up to her waist. When they arrived at the barn, the door was blocked by a pile of white snow. Papa and Alex grabbed shovels and quickly removed the barrier. The gusts of wind and snow were so strong that the cold pierced right through Kathleen's clothes, despite all the layers she wore. But the struggle was worth it; she was glad to be out of the house and she loved helping with the barn chores. Everyone kept so busy there was no time for her confession. Lindsay taught her how to milk Clover. She was their gentlest milk cow. But best of all, after all the chores were done, Kathleen had time to pet Doll's velvety nose and run her hand down the filly's soft coat.

When they got back to the house, Kathleen had planned to tell Bruce and Lindsay about Bruiser before dinner, but she just could not bring herself to tell them yet. Besides, Bruiser was getting better each day and it would be much easier to tell them if Kathleen had the assurance that he would pull through.

But Papa was right, not telling her cousins was making life more difficult. She felt herself withdrawing and

found that she was spending more and more time reading her books and less time with Lindsay. They seemed to have so little in common. Kathleen felt lonely and longed for Lucy. Maybe when school started things would be different.

The blizzard lasted so long that the start of school was delayed. At first Kathleen was disappointed; but now she determined to study twice as hard on her own. For the first time, she was truly grateful that her parents had given her schoolbooks for Christmas.

Finally, she could see God's plan. It would have been monotonous to be cooped up in the house without any books to challenge her mind or imagination. At the time she had been so ungrateful for her Christmas presents, but now she was glad.

She had been mortified when Lindsay had said she did not see any reason to attend school. But over the past few days she could see Lindsay's interest growing. Lindsay had even asked if she could join her whenever she studied. Before long, Kathleen felt sure that Lindsay had a secret desire to learn.

Kathleen again offered to help Lindsay catch up in her studies and assured her that she would do just fine. At first Lindsay was a bit hesitant and seemed embarrassed at how far behind she was, but with each new day, Lindsay's courage grew. Now, after several days, Kathleen noticed that Lindsay actually enjoyed their study times together.

Old Bruiser

On this particular evening, Kathleen paused from figuring a math equation and looked up at the oil-burning lamp on the kitchen table. She stared into the flickering light for a long time.

"What are you thinking about?" Lindsay asked after a few minutes.

"I was thinking about how strange it was for me when I first came here to study by lamplight. Back in the city all I had to do was flip a switch, and the whole room lit up. But I think candlelight and firelight are growing on me. It is almost—well, it's kind of dreamy and whimsical." She leaned toward Lindsay. "Imagine that we are two princesses studying in a faraway land, with the firelight warming the cold castle walls and casting its shimmering light on the pages of our books, illuminating the dramatic tale we are reading. Perhaps we are reading the tragic story of an ancestor who was held captive far from the land she called home . . . far from everything familiar . . ." Kathleen's voice faded, as she thought about Lucy and the many hours they had spent in the tree house in Kirk's Woods, and the night they were scared out of their wits by a peacock.

"I can't say that I can picture myself as a princess studying in a castle—in fact, I've never imagined anything of the like." Lindsay scratched her forehead with her pencil. "It is an unusual—yet pretty thought."

Kathleen put her chin in her hand and sighed. Lindsay was too practical to understand. "I was also thinking about my friends back home. I try not to, but sometimes I wonder what my classmates are studying right now—I don't want to fall behind. And I also miss Lucy. Actually, I miss her a lot." Kathleen's voice caught and her eyes burned.

Lindsay placed her hand on Kathleen's. "I'm sorry you had to leave your friends. I can't imagine moving away from the farm—not even for a little while. I've never left home for more than a day trip to town. But I am thankful that God sent you here. I've never really had a friend near my own age, and I didn't realize how very much I longed for one—that is, not until you came."

Lindsay's words penetrated the very depths of Kathleen's heart. How selfish she'd been, always thinking of herself and how much she missed her friends. She'd never once considered that Lindsay might need a friend.

Was it that she didn't think she and Lindsay had much in common? Or was it her guilty conscience over Bruiser that had kept her from getting close to Lindsay? Kathleen decided she had put off telling her about the dog incident long enough.

"Lindsay, there's something I have to tell you." As she talked, she prayed that God would give her the right words. She was so nervous, she couldn't even look at Lindsay's face for fear of what she'd see written there. Instead, she played with a drop of wax left by a candle.

When she was done, there was silence. She finally looked up. Amazement was what she saw in her cousin's eyes.

"You shot Bruiser from that distance? Wow!"

"I didn't mean to. I thought he was a wolf."

"I can't hit any of the targets that Bruce puts up, no matter how hard I try. Bruce was right. You are an Annie Oakley."

"You're not upset?"

"Well, maybe a little for not telling me sooner."

Kathleen felt lighter, freer, and now wished she'd been more honest with Lindsay. "I'm sorry I didn't tell you sooner. I was so embarrassed—I thought for sure you'd make fun of me."

Lindsay looked at her blankly. "Why would I do that?"

"Because it just proves that I'm a city girl who doesn't fit in here."

"But you're such a quick learner. Besides, you're younger than me and yet you know so much. I'm the one who feels awkward around you."

"You do?" Kathleen laughed. "But you're so good at everything. You can milk a cow and ride a horse . . ." She stopped and the girls studied one another. At that moment they both realized that they were good at different things and had been comparing themselves to each other.

They had a good laugh and promised to not let their strengths and weaknesses get in the way of their friendship.

When Kathleen went to bed that night, she thanked God for His wisdom and for just the right moment to talk to Lindsay. Now, she just had to tell Bruce.

Kathleen's Unforgettable Winter

Kathleen removed the heavy blanket that Aunt Elizabeth had hung over Lindsay's bedroom window to keep the heat in. The winds had subsided, and the relentless snow had stopped. Kathleen could hardly wait to look outside.

The sun shone brilliantly, revealing a glinting, snow-covered world. Drifts piled nearly fourteen feet high in some places. In others they stood only five feet deep. Uncle John, Papa, and the boys were down below shoveling a path through the deep banks to the barn. It looked like they were creating a deep canyon as the snow was over their heads. Kathleen looked around the yard; all the outbuildings were buried to their roofs in the white stuff.

"All I can see beyond the barn and farmyard is a huge rolling sea of sparkling snow." Kathleen squinted, trying to see anything that looked familiar. But everything seemed different under the layer of snow.

Lindsay joined her at the window. "My Pa figures that it will take several days of shoveling before we're able to move around freely. He says that by the time we've shoveled the snow from the driveway, the county road may be plowed and packed enough to take the sleigh out. I hope he's right — there's nothing better than a sleigh ride on a day like this."

Everyone had cabin fever, and they were delighted and relieved to help dig paths through the deep snow

and venture into the pure white beyond. Even Old Bruiser started to scamper about the house and let out frisky yelps like a pup. Uncle John chuckled and said it was obvious that his shoulder wound was well on the road to recovery and that with love and attention he had turned out to be a nice dog after all.

Kathleen was relieved to see that Bruiser was healing, but now she dreaded returning him to his owner. Her prayers were more focused on asking God to give her the courage to face Mr. Johnston. Not only did she still have to tell Bruce that she'd shot Bruiser, she had to confess to his owner.

The next several days went by quickly, and before she knew it, Uncle John announced at dinner what she had been dreading.

"By tomorrow morning, the roads should be packed enough to use our sleigh," Uncle John said, as he cut into a venison steak from Bruce's deer. "I think it's high time we returned Old Bruiser to his owner. No doubt Mr. Johnston is quite anxious to know what happened to his watchdog. He will be happy to know that he is still alive and not buried beneath ten feet of snow."

The following morning, Kathleen stood in the barn anxiously breaking up little pieces of straw while she watched Alex hitch the draft horses, Dan and Daisy, to the sleigh. She wondered what Mr. Johnston was like. Would he believe her story? Alex invited Bruce and Lindsay to join Kathleen and him. "After we drop off

Mr. Johnston's dog, we'll check on our neighbors to see how they fared in the storm."

Kathleen dreaded facing Mr. Johnston, but she knew she had to apologize for shooting his dog.

"Are we going to stop by the Williamses' house?" asked Lindsay. "I've been so wanting to meet them—I hear they have a daughter near my age." Lindsay ran toward the house for her heavy wrap and hood.

"Sure, if we can make it through the snow banks," Alex called after her.

Bruce scratched his head as if deep in thought. "Do you suppose we should bring some food and blankets just in case they weren't as prepared for the storm as we were? They just moved up here from Alabama, and they've never experienced weather quite like this." Bruce had a caring expression on his face that Kathleen had never noticed before.

Maybe she had misjudged him. Could it be that Bruce had a tender, compassionate heart hidden behind that brave, strong exterior? Maybe he'd understand how a girl from the city could accidentally mistake a dog for a wolf?

Kathleen helped him load supplies into the sleigh. It was red and black and large enough to seat six people comfortably. It reminded Kathleen of a picture she had seen on a Christmas card.

They bundled up Old Bruiser and put him in a bed they had prepared at the back of the sleigh. Then they climbed in, Bruce and Alex on the front seats,

Lindsay and Kathleen on the back ones. With a sudden jolt, they were off behind the two strong draft horses.

Kathleen grabbed the seat in front of her. "Whoa! Do they usually go this fast?"

"They've been cooped up in the barn," Lindsay laughed lightheartedly. "Don't worry, Alex and Bruce are great with horses."

Kathleen hoped so. The horses' hooves sent snow flying through the air. The harness's bells jingled as they trotted through the deep drifts. She surely did not want to end up in a ditch somewhere.

Before long Kathleen relaxed. The bells chimed merrily and thick clouds of steam burst from the horses' nostrils.

"There's the Johnston's house," Bruce said, pointing at a small, unpainted one-story house with snow up to its roof. The driveway had been shoveled and there was a narrow path to the front door. As they neared the house, Kathleen could see another path veering off to the side of the house and she figured it led around the back of the house to the barn.

The enjoyment of the ride suddenly ended. It was time to face Mr. Johnston. She stared at the weathered old farmhouse and tried to imagine what kind of people lived inside. Kathleen could feel her hands sweating inside her mittens. She felt both embarrassed and scared, but mostly just terrified at the thought of how Mr. Johnston might respond.

Kathleen's Unforgettable Winter

Alex turned to Bruce before climbing out of the sleigh. "We won't be here long. Why don't you and Lindsay wait here, and I'll take Kathleen with me."

Kathleen felt relieved. Now Bruce need never know that she was the one who shot Bruiser.

"Why are you taking her with you?" asked Bruce. "I should go with you."

Alex looked at Kathleen and she realized that now was the time to tell Bruce about Bruiser.

When she was done, Kathleen fully expected Bruce to lose respect for her, but instead he said, "You should have told me sooner that you were the one who shot the dog. I don't think any less of you — it's an easy mistake to make. Bruiser looks like a large coyote or a wolf. I just hope Mr. Johnston is as understanding when you tell him. You've got a lot of courage. I sure don't envy you right now."

Even though Kathleen was relieved at Bruce's response, his remarks about Mr. Johnston made her nervous. If Bruce was concerned about what Mr. Johnston might think, she must really have reason to worry.

Alex helped Kathleen out of the sleigh. She straightened her shoulders and, despite the butterflies in her stomach, did her best to smile.

Alex gathered the dog into his arms and Kathleen followed him up the shoveled pathway to the door. Alex knocked on the weathered wooden door. He looked at Kathleen and winked. He must have seen the anxiety on her face.

Old Bruiser

"It will be okay. I'll do the talking. All you need to do is be your sweet self and apologize."

The door opened slowly and a middle-aged woman peered out. Her graying hair was pulled back in a tight bun behind her ears. She looked like the perfect picture of a classic old maid taken out of a storybook a century earlier.

"Move yourselves on in—all our heat's getting out. Glad to see that storm didn't harm you none," she muttered as she opened the door wider and motioned them inside the one-room farmhouse. Kathleen quickly scanned the bare wood floor and walls, the shabby couch near the fireplace, and the small table, cluttered with dirty dishes and old newspapers.

"What you got in that bundle?" a gruff voice called from across the room.

Kathleen looked toward the man she assumed to be Mr. Johnston. She opened her mouth to say something, but nothing came out. Thankfully, Alex came to the rescue.

"Well, sir, if I'm not mistaken, it is Old Bruiser, your dog." Alex gently placed the dog on the floor and unwrapped the old blanket they had bundled him in. "He's wounded, sir, but looks like he'll pull through fine."

"Bruiser!" Mr. Johnston's face lit up. "Why, I thought for sure he was dead. Let me take a look at him." Bruiser wagged his tail as Mr. Johnston rushed across the room. Kathleen thought she caught a glimpse of a smile hidden somewhere beneath his gruff face.

"That's Bruiser, all right," Mrs. Johnston said from her rocking chair, which she'd sat in after she'd let them in. Her face, which looked as if it never changed expression, had taken on a look of astonishment.

Mr. Johnston examined Bruiser's wound, then stood and patted Alex on the back. "Some fool neighbor must have shot him—probably that worthless Southern family. They just moved to these parts, you know—but he's a tough old dog. Thanks for saving him."

Kathleen caught her breath when she saw the contempt in the man's eyes when he referred to the Southern family. How was she going to explain that she was the guilty one?

Alex shifted his weight, squared his shoulders, and looked Mr. Johnston straight in the eye. "No, sir, leave the Williams family out of it. I'm afraid it was an accident, and it is entirely my family's fault. You see, sir, Bruce decided to take my cousin Kathleen hunting for the first time. She is visiting from the city." Alex put his hand on Kathleen's shoulder.

Mr. Johnston looked at her with a shocked expression, as if he hadn't realized she was even in the room until then.

"You mean—you're not telling me Bruce shot my dog to impress this little girl, are you?"

Kathleen noticed the color rising in Mr. Johnston's face, and she was not about to allow him to think badly of Bruce.

Kathleen stepped forward. "No, sir! I shot your dog," Kathleen blurted. "I mean—I didn't want to shoot him—I wanted . . . or rather, I thought he was a wolf. Bruce had gone to track a deer, and when your dog came trotting out of the woods toward me, I was sure he was going to attack me—I shot him out of self defense. I honestly didn't know it was your dog, and I am so sorry."

There was a long silence and Mr. Johnston's face turned from shock to confusion, and then red with anger. He stared hard at the floor as if he were trying to decide what to say.

Kathleen's tongue felt like cotton in her mouth and her hand shook nervously.

"Well, now you've said your piece." Mrs. Johnston stood. "You better be on your way. My husband and I are beholden to you for returning our dog." She hurried them to the door and quickly shut it behind them before Kathleen had time to look at Mr. Johnston again to see if he was still mad at her.

Alex took a deep breath as they walked back to the sleigh. "Phew! That's over. They're such an odd couple; you never know how they'll react to anything. Mr. Johnston is known far and wide for his temper. The fact that he didn't blow up is a good sign. I feel pretty sure everything will be just fine," Alex said, climbing back up on the sleigh.

Kathleen had her doubts, but decided to take Alex's word for it. She was just thankful that her apology was over and that she could move on.

The Rescue

*The eternal God is your refuge, and underneath
are the everlasting arms.*
DEUTERONOMY 33:27

Kathleen tried to erase the memory of Mr. Johnston's angry face as they drove to the Williamses', but her vivid imagination replayed what could have happened if he had decided to blow up. Kathleen sighed. She would have to add this in her note to Lucy. She had been compiling page after page of her adventures since she arrived at the farm—if she did not get it mailed soon, Lucy would be receiving a book rather than a letter.

She felt bad that she had not sent Lucy any letters yet. When she had promised to write often, she did not realize she could only send letters when the family went into town for supplies. She could not wait to go to the post office. Surely there would be a letter waiting for her from Lucy. She so wanted to know how her dear friend was doing.

The Rescue

As they neared the Williamses' one-story farm-house, Kathleen was surprised to see that no one had dug a path through the snow to the front door, like at the Johnstons'. The house was still buried beneath the snow, with the exception of the ridge line along the rooftop that poked through the otherwise smooth land-scape. Alex urged the horses forward.

"There's no smoke coming out of the chimney. They must be in trouble," Bruce said, pointing toward the roof. When they were within earshot, the boys called out repeatedly to see if there was any sign of life. "Hello, anyone home?" The only answers were hungry moos coming from the direction of the barn.

"It will take some digging to get to the barn door, but the cows can wait. We need to make sure there is no one in this house first." Alex pulled the horses to a stop.

Bruce reached under the seat and brought out a shovel. He leaped from the sleigh and started digging through the snow.

Alex climbed down from the sleigh and began dig-ging with his hands. Kathleen and Lindsay followed his example and it wasn't long before they were nearing the base of the door.

"Girls, there is no telling what we'll find once we are inside," Bruce warned. "I think you two should start digging a path to the barn so we can get those cows fed." The look on his face and the gravity in his voice made Kathleen shudder.

133

"You don't think that the people in there froze to death, do you?" Lindsay asked with wide eyes.

Just then they heard a shuffle on the other side of the door, followed by a muffled voice. "Glory be to God! Someone is here to help us. He has answered our prayers at last."

"Is everyone all right in there?" Alex called into the keyhole and then placed his ear to it, trying to hear the feeble reply.

"You came just in time. The missus and baby won't make it much longer without food and warmth."

"Girls," Alex waved at them, "fetch the food and blankets from the sleigh." He and Bruce dug at the snow bank surrounding the door with renewed energy.

By the time Kathleen and Lindsay were back with their arms full of supplies, the boys had entered the house. It took some time for Kathleen's eyes to adjust to the darkness on the inside. But soon she could see a small room with lots of children huddled together in the corner. Kathleen noticed that they were a black family.

The father, Mr. Williams, explained to Alex and Bruce how the storm had taken them by surprise. The man kept shaking Alex's and Bruce's hands and repeating his thanks over and over.

Kathleen looked from the grateful father to the shivering children in the corner and took action right away. "Lindsay, I'll warm the children with blankets, and you find some kindling outside to start a fire in the stove.

The sooner we get that broth warmed up the better."
Kathleen was surprised at her own confidence, but she
knew something needed to be done fast.

"Great work, Kathleen!" Alex said. "Mrs. Williams
is in the back room. She'll need some blankets too. Mr.
Williams and I are going outside to dig our way through
to the woodpile."

Bruce grabbed a blanket and headed to the back
room, where they could hear the faint cry of a baby.
Kathleen turned her attention to the five shivering children huddled in the corner. There were three girls and
two boys.

"Th—thank you, ma'am," a timid girl, about
Kathleen's own age, managed to say through chattering
teeth. Her hair was done up in small braids that hung
randomly across her forehead. At the end of each one
was tied a neat white bow made out of cut-up flour
sacks. They framed her small face, making her look
somewhat angelic, except for the dark brown, frightened eyes that gazed back at her. Kathleen's heart went
out to the girl. She did not understand why she was
scared. It was almost as if the girl was unsure of
whether or not they came as friends.

"You don't have to call me ma'am. My name's
Kathleen." Kathleen tucked the blanket around the girl.
The other four children huddled even closer to their
older sister, trying to soak up all the heat they could get.

"Yes, ma'am. Whatever you say," the girl responded.

Kathleen wondered if she had heard what she said.

135

Kathleen's Unforgettable Winter

"I hear you're new to Ohio. Me too. Don't you worry one little bit, my cousins are the kindest of people, and we won't leave until you are all safe and sound." Kathleen took a deep breath. She spoke so fast, trying to ease the frightened children, that she ran out of air. Kathleen noticed the oldest girl's eyes turned from fear to curiosity to total surprise all within those few sentences. Kathleen smiled and headed to the kitchen to help Lindsay with the food.

As she helped cut slices of homemade bread and thick cuts of smoked ham, for the first time Kathleen felt like a part of the family and that she was actually needed instead of just a distant relative that dropped in from another world and lifestyle. What her papa had said now began to make sense. Before she had been absorbed with herself, her problems, her pride—worrying about being liked and accepted. But now that she was looking out for the interests of those around her and looking for ways to serve others, she not only felt needed, but her heart was fuller than it had been in years.

12

Lucy

Wait for the LORD; be strong and take heart and wait for the LORD.
PSALM 27:14

Around the dinner table that evening, everyone wanted to hear about the Williams family. Bruce told how he found the baby crying in the back room with Mrs. Williams, who was so weak from undernourishment that she could barely lift her head.

"I wasn't really sure what to do with the baby, but the little fellow looked hungry, and I knew that babies like milk, so I asked Lindsay to mind him while I headed to the barn with the shovel. It took me some time to dig my way to the barn door, but I couldn't get the helpless look of the mama's face and the faint, hungry cry of the baby out of my mind. When I finally did get in there, I don't know who was more relieved—the milk cows or me. She looked like she'd been needing a good milking for a few days. She's a skinny cow though. I think we should bring them some extra grain for their livestock or they won't have any animals come spring."

Kathleen sat in wonder as she listened to her cousin. She definitely had misjudged him. He may have been a bit ornery when he was young, and a tease at times, but he had a big heart that was tender and kind. They talked and marveled at the unique events of the day until late into the evening.

Later, as Lindsay washed and Kathleen helped dry the dishes with a dishrag made from cut-up flour sacks, she thought of the Williamses' oldest daughter, Sharly, and the white flour sack bows that were tied around the end of each braid. Kathleen could not figure out why Sharly was so frightened of her. She had never had that effect on anyone before.

Kathleen was about to explain her concerns to Mama, when Papa walked into the kitchen.

"While you were out helping the neighbors today, your uncle and I took Grandpa's two-seater sleigh and the bay gelding, Lightning, into town. Uncle John needed a few things from the hardware store, and I was anxious to use the pay telephone at the general store to call some of my contacts in Fort Wayne," Papa said.

"Your contacts? Does that mean you might have a job?" Kathleen almost dropped the dish she was drying.

"No, there is nothing definite, but there are some leads that require me to make an immediate trip to Fort Wayne to investigate. And considering how fast the snow was melting on the roads today, I may even be

able to leave tomorrow." Papa rubbed his chin in an attempt to hide his smile.

"Oh, Papa, are you serious? Can I go with you?" Kathleen waved her dish around and Mama grabbed it out of her hand.

"Careful there, young lady."

Kathleen looked at Lindsay, who was standing at the sink, listening intently. "Can I bring Lindsay with me? I would love to show her Fort Wayne and introduce her to Lucy, and then we could go to my tree house and everything!"

"That would be wonderful at some point, but I don't think this trip is the best timing," said Papa. "I will only be there a few short days, and with travel time, the two of you would miss your first week at school. We can't have that, now, can we?"

"I don't want to miss school. But can we take Lindsay to Fort Wayne sometime soon?" Kathleen tried to hide her disappointment. She knew Papa was right, that she should not miss any more days at school, but even so, Kathleen could not help but feel somewhat saddened at the thought of Papa visiting home without her.

"I do have one thing that might brighten your evening. Your uncle and I just happened to stop by the post office and . . ." He took a white envelope out of his pocket.

"A letter from Lucy!" Kathleen exclaimed. She put her dish towel down and rushed over to his side.

"Well, you're right about the letter, but it isn't from Lucy. It seems Freddie Schmitt has beat Lucy in

sending you your first letter." Papa grinned and affectionately ran his finger down Kathleen's freckled nose like he always did when he was teasing her. Kathleen took the letter.

"Freddie Schmitt? Why would he be writing me?" Kathleen examined the handwriting on the envelope, looking for answers. Why hadn't Lucy written?

"You know, I asked myself that very same question. I cannot imagine why a nice young man like Freddie would want to write an attractive, smart girl like you," Papa said with a twinkle in his eye.

Kathleen knew what he was implying. Even though Papa was just teasing her, she felt her cheeks growing warm. "Oh, Papa! We are just friends." She shoved the letter into her apron pocket and turned to put the dishes away, hoping to prove her disinterest. But her mind was spinning.

She hoped Freddie did not think they were more than friends. She had decided long ago not to have a beau until she was ready to get married and that was years from now.

For a brief moment, Kathleen envisioned what they would both be like when they were eighteen. Freddie would be tall and a doctor like his father. Would he be the person she'd marry? She blushed that she was even thinking about him in that way.

Kathleen hurried to finish her kitchen chores and then stole quietly away to the privacy of the room she shared with Lindsay. Her hands shook as she broke

the seal. She was so eager to hear news from home —
even if it was from Freddie and not Lucy.

She carefully opened the letter and eagerly read his
note written in fine penmanship:

Dear Kathleen,

As I feared, Fort Wayne has not been the same since you left. I have no one to challenge me to snowball fights or keep me on my toes in class. Worst of all, the weather has been gray and dismal since the day you left — I think you took the sunshine with you. Before, our class had Lucy's and your bright smiles to cheer the cloudy days, but suddenly you both have vanished.

I hope you don't mind me writing you. I thought you might be a little homesick. Also, I can only imagine how anxious you are about Lucy, so my intention in sending you this letter is to express to you that your friends back home are thinking of you. I know that if Lucy's health were to permit, she would be writing you.

This might not make things easier on you, but I think you should know that my papa told the Meiers to send for Lucy's brother, Peter. He came immediately and is now at Lucy's bedside. Papa says he has been at her bedside night and day since he arrived — he's never seen a more devoted brother.

Feel free to write, if ever you are lonely or need to hear from your chum back home.

Your friend,
Fred

Kathleen's Unforgettable Winter

Kathleen read the lines of the note over and over until she could have no doubt of the meaning. The letter dropped from her fingers, and she stared blankly at the lamplight flickering on the wall.

Lucy was sick. She had been sick all this time and she had known nothing about it. Freddie obviously thought she knew or else he would have given her more details. Dr. Schmitt sent for Peter—surely that didn't mean—surely she hadn't already—

The letter had been written over a week ago.

Dear Lord, please don't let Lucy die. Please, please let me see her again.

What is wrong with Lucy?
Will Kathleen get to see her?
Or is it too late?

Find out in:

KATHLEEN'S ABIDING HOPE
Book Three

ABOUT THE AUTHOR

*A*uthor Tracy Leininger Craven is known for capturing the stories of real-life Christian heroines from America's past in historical fiction books. She is the author of many titles, including:

- **Alone Yet Not Alone**
  The Story of Barbara and Regina Leininger
- **Unfading Beauty**
  The Story of Dolley Madison
- **The Land Beyond the Setting Sun**
  The Story of Sacagawea

- **Nothing Can Separate Us**
  The Story of Nan Harper
- **A Light Kindled**
  The Story of Priscilla Mullins
- **Our Flag Was Still There**
  The Story of the Star-Spangled Banner

Tracy Leininger Craven loves history and the people whose lives have left an indelible impression on our country's heritage. She is also inspired by the testimony of God's faithfulness through seemingly impossible circumstances. Her stories of real people come alive and serve to mentor and inspire a new generation of readers.

Tracy, her husband David, and their daughters Elaina Hope and Evangelina Lilly live in the beautiful Texas Hill Country.

For more information, visit www.hisseasons.com or call (210) 490-2101.